T0094508

# ARIADNE IN THE GROTESQUE LABYRINTH

# ARIADNE IN THE GROTESQUE LABYRINTH

### SALVADOR ESPRIU

Translated by Rowan Ricardo Phillips

Dalkey Archive Press
Champaign • Dublin • London

Originally published in Catalan as *Ariadna al laberint grotesc*
© Estate of Salvador Espriu, 1975
Edicions 62, S.A., Edicions 62
Peu de la Creu, 4, 08001 Barcelona
www.edicions62.cat
Translation copyright © 2012 by Rowan Ricardo Phillips
First edition, 2012
All rights reserved

Library of Congress Cataloging-in-Publication Data

Espriu, Salvador.
  [Ariadna al laberint grotesc. English]
  Ariadne in the grotesque labyrinth / Salvador Espriu ; translated by Rowan Ricardo Phillips. -- 1st ed.
    p. cm.
  "Originally published in Catalan as Ariadna al laberint grotesc, 1935, by La Rosa del Vents, Barcelona"--T.p. verso.
  ISBN 978-1-56478-772-9 (pbk. : acid-free paper) -- ISBN 978-1-56478-732-3 (cloth : acid-free paper)
  I. Phillips, Rowan Ricardo. II. Title.
  PC3941.E84A913 2012
  849'.9352--dc23
                        2012013726

Partially funded by a grant from the Illinois Arts Council, a state agency

The Catalan Literature Series is published in cooperation with the Institut Ramon Llull, a public consortium responsible for the promotion of Catalan language and culture abroad.

www.dalkeyarchive.com

Cover: design and composition by Mikhail Iliatov

Printed on permanent/durable acid-free paper and bound in the United States of America

# Contents

# A Note on the Text and the Translation

Salvador Espriu continued to add stories—six more in all—to the various editions of *Ariadna al laberint grotesc* that saw the light of day between the book's first appearance in 1935 and the author's death in 1985, a period which spanned the rise, fall, and aftermath of Franco's dictatorship. The last of these stories, the statement-of-purpose tinged "The Young Man and the Old Man," was inserted by Espriu at the beginning of the book: the last becoming first. Both in form and function the prefatory "The Young Man and the Old Man" is a far more faithful introduction to the temperament of this masterpiece of Catalan literature than my prosaic intrusion into your enjoyment of it could ever be. An introduction to *Ariadne in the Grotesque Labyrinth* could occupy four times the pages of this slender text; and you, reader, will feel at times as though you could use one; but Espriu is interested in your being—or at least feeling—lost, and in the threads that lead you toward feeling less so.

*Ariadne in the Grotesque Labyrinth* lifts the specious reality of the surfaces of Espriu's world to reveal the awkward, kaleidoscopic reality that exists beneath it. Among modern writers, Espriu is the one who most abides by the inner logic of his own world-making. Hence, many of the lusciously-named characters who will appear in these stories (and subsequently re-appear, interrupting narratives seemingly at whim with a syncopated nonchalance) also appear in numerous other stories and poems within Espriu's oeuvre. Similarly, the invented names of the locations in these stories will be unfamiliar to those new to Espriu's work. They are as follows: "Sinera", which is "Arenys" backwards—Espriu is from Arenys de Mar, a coastal town about an hour north of Barcelona; "Lavínia" for Barcelona; "Alfaranja" for Catalunya; and Konilòsia for Spain. This last place-name plays on the Catalan word for rabbit, "conill," and the name given to Spain by the arriving Carthaginians around 300 B.C.: "Ispania"—"land of the rabbits."

What is a grotesque labyrinth? The adjective evokes Valle-Inclán's theater of the grotesque. As both style and ontology, the grotesque offers torment and tragedy to its audience within a torqued, feral sense of reality. An admixture, at its best, of pathos and irony, this grotesque work of art is a daedal refraction of what had once been assumed real; and in this sense it offers the possibility of hope to those willing to read through its reflection, its refraction, its torqued and necessary otherness.

However, Espriu's labyrinth is not only grotesque, it is also allegorical, a place and structure conceived of as both condition and cure. Class lines are constantly crossed; every form of betrayal—even the betrayal of genre—looms; quietly, a bestiary builds; anachronistic slang and the Caló language of the Iberian gypsies perforate the text. There is much betwixt and between, harshness and smoothness, crudeness and elegance, nonsense and sense, a sense of feeling found and of feeling quite lost all at once in this wonderful book. There is a strong baroque tinge to Espriu's prose, the pulse of which in particular rises and falls in such a way as to evoke a style both fashionable and unfashionable, historical and ahistorical, stern and yet welcoming to purple patches. I have tried to remain faithful to that pulse by producing something in English that is close to the tone and temperament of Espriu's Catalan (and Castillian Spanish and gypsy Caló). For readers who find themselves lost as they read, I ask that you consider it part of the process of winding through the labyrinth; or blame the translator.

Two final notes.

I maintained the symbols [«] and [»] as they were prevalent throughout the text but for the most part distinguished in their use from quotation marks.

And finally, I would like to dedicate this translation to Jordi Royo Seubas.

# The Young Man and the Old Man

This little book was begun by a twenty-one-year-old who didn't get along well with himself and was pretty hard on everyone else. A sixty-one-year-old who fails to get along well with himself and attempts—from a distance—to understand everyone else has finished it, perhaps. Perhaps. Quite a few things, and not all of them adverse, have happened during the intervening forty years. Things that are, or should be, understood and remembered.

During that time this little book was remolded again and again, without end. Perhaps this effort wasn't worth the trouble. No doubt the extremely tedious labor was in vain. But both the young man and the old man coincide in their affirmation that this, and all of the other works brought to life by the two of them—as well as those works (who knows?) that the old man may still have time to realize—are merely ephemeral tokens of a strange and difficult apprenticeship set within the perplex coherence of a labyrinth. And in this affirmation one would like to see, with a benevolent irony—an irony that seems rather grateful, from this vantage—a sarcastic skillfulness, the lightning rod of false modesty, when it merely reflects an uncomfortable, obsessive, and literal truth.

All the echoes of *noucentisme* and *post-noucentisme* that this little book contained, that could have been pointed out here and there, have been extinguished, bit by bit, in systematic order. If some trace of them remains within the diction and syntax, it's been kept expressly for its grotesque clink.

It's the same book, and yet, at the same time, another. The young man didn't err completely; and it's out of bounds to claim that all of the old man's suggestions were right. Which is why the old man has maintained in his mind, and so often returned to, that first distant draft of the text. He preserves from it a certain ingenuousness more apparent than real; and he has eliminated whatever imprecise or coarse expressions it contained. The young man suspected, and the old man firmly believes, that anything can and should be said without falling head first into the sort of dull and jejune shoddiness that industriously seduces so many talented pens—the most indigestible leftovers from rhetoric's waste bin.

Nothing in this book has been invented. Everything told in it happened, one way or another. The young man possessed, and the old man preserves, a precise memory, an ear and vision diligent and acute. But neither of the two has benefited, not even on the rebound, from the brilliant, utterly enviable subtleties of the imagination.

This little book forms an essential unity. Thus, the hypothetical curious reader should read these prose pieces according to the very deliberate order in which they appear. Some short stories here serve to round off and stress the meanings of others, as well as functioning as links. They also present clear situations and characters that will be the objects of other stories.

The young man has vanished, of course. His heir, the old man, is still here. But the only award he's attained is a glacial serenity. His profits are such that he'll never complain.

«Let's leave him cold, if not lukewarm,» Senyora Magdalena Blasi said, toning things down. «And let's not waste time trying to figure him out, because we'd immediately raise his temperature, with a consequent alteration of the costly product.»

«The old man desires no distinction, doesn't want to belong to any institution, to any organization or faction,» Salom the ventriloquist intervened.

«Either of them now opposed to the genuine interests of a country that cannot allow itself the foolish luxury of any type of dispute,» lectured the acknowledged patriot Carranza i Brofegat.

«The old man,» continued the ventriloquist, «does not want to figure on any list, nor in any ambiguous, sentimentalizing document. He wants neither to collaborate nor to go anywhere. He doesn't want to be manipulated any longer by alleged—and more often than not indelicate—affections, those pressures to which he was forced to yield himself with mild but always lucid contempt.»

«He's played it off long enough,» Senyora Magdalena Blasi responded.

«The game, if indeed there has been a game,» Salom started up again, «is forever over. Before the old man lies the rough slope of his duty—either uphill or down. And he's taken on tasks that he'll seek to complete, whether or not they're to his liking.»

«If the old man tends to swell up, I can't deny that he cares,» added Senyora Magdalena Blasi.

«The old man no longer wishes to present to the public,» said

Salom, «even a single commodity that is someone else's—be it more or less intelligent, inspired, sophisticated, or authentic. He does not want to judge anyone, or respond to polls, or suffer through any more absent-minded, reiterative, inelegant, monotonous interrogations . . . unless they are, for example, a matter for the authorities or for a judge. He is in neither the physical nor the moral condition to maintain any type of regular correspondence. If he does not love very much and does not hate at all, then he profoundly respects everyone. In exchange he requests that his solitude be respected, without exception. He supposes that is not too much to ask.»

«Yes, it's definitely too much to ask!» murmured Senyora Magdalena Blasi, between yawns. «And he'll have to readjust—by force, if you please—his plans. On the other hand, this gloomy old man would willingly thumb, in his premature niche, through newspapers and magazines.»

«Let's see if these brief paragraphs,» psalmed the ventriloquist, «excluding all kinds of haughtiness without, however, excluding the opportunity for it, end up being intelligible. For this skeptical man, whom neither gold nor terror nor any flattery could buy or soften, was taught according to norms of rigid courtesy no longer incumbent. And he has been quite vulnerable, thanks to this gross defect in his education. He has liberally given away his time, but can no longer afford to lose even a mere morsel of it. He owes only that to his conscience—which, if it didn't seem pretentious, would at least qualify as strict, though also independent and free.»

«He's a scaredy-cat and a softy!» Senyora Magdalena Blasi yellowed. «Everything, leaving aside the eternal mysteries of inflation, has a price,» she smiled, with good reason. «If the old man exalts himself it's a trick of age. But he's not so old. He exaggerates. I'm older than he is,» Senyora Magdalena Blasi impartially confirmed.

«Along the curve of the biological and the essential, nothing is fixed,» stated Doctor Robuster i Tramusset, with blanched eyes.

«The feedback from my naked words,» concluded Salom, «does not by any means have to affect this tired man incapable of deception and self-pity. If he wanted, he would pray for those who are his friends, and those who are not his friends alike, to be saved.»

«These precautions won't stop them from skinning him,» said Senyora Magdalena Blasi scornfully, as she receded.

In the little book discussed above, along with a number of dialogues and monologues, oddities and extravagances, there is some gipsyism and a very few neologisms and semantic leaps, and the vocabulary and discourse are subject, not without restrained rebellion, to the dictated and codified laws and lists of the Institute of Catalan Studies, some of whose pressing rules will have to be modified and revised bit by bit. We find ourselves today between two fires: on the one hand a rigid and paralytic purism; on the other an irresponsible and inadmissible patois. Perhaps one will have to insist on searching, between extreme and extreme, for the equilibrium of a middle ground. The man who writes these lines ought not to instruct anyone, does not want to instruct anyone, nor can he instruct anyone. Because he has no authority. Because—if by some tactical miscalculation a speck of it is attributed to him—as everything has been sung, recited, or told, and everyone has forgotten everything, nothing should have to be repeated. Because the old man has learned that «many words that have been lost will be born again, and many more now honored will be lost.» Because he understood, through his dangerously intimate contradictions, that «the language of art's future is always an unknown language.»

S. E.
*Barcelona, 25 July 1974*

Many years ago, Ariadne guided you, for half an hour, through a simple but singular labyrinth. She went ahead of you. You walked among odd voices and shapes. If you felt faint you could sit down in a peaceful corner of your own choosing. You didn't have to encounter the Minotaur. The labyrinth was insignificant, harmless, for tourists. When you tired, diligent Ariadne would attend to you and, at utter peace, show you the point of departure. But if she sensed you were feeling bold, she benevolently left you the illusion of having discovered the way out on your own—though without her you would have been lost. Ariadne was discreet; she barely spoke, insinuating the path for you to follow with a soft gesture. Ariadne was modest; and I advised you how best to reward her: you had to invite her, once she got off work, to tea and a dance. If you were to her liking—educated in Germany, Ariadne, was a romantic—and you requited the feelings of that affectionate girl, then it was good to remember that Naxos was always at hand. Upon waking, the sleeping beauty complained of the silence, but was soon consoled: just off the coast, Dionysus gathered Ariadne's destiny. Hard times followed nevertheless; and that destiny was ruined, as was mine, as were perhaps all of ours.

# Little-Teresa-Who-Went-Down-the-Stairs

*To Maria Aurèlia Capmany and Llorenç Villalonga, in homage*
*and with the promise to never revise this story again.*

## I

«It doesn't count, it doesn't count yet: you're looking. You have to close your eyes and you have to turn your back to us and face toward Santa Maria. But you have to focus on the route first, it goes through Carrer dels Corders, past Carrer de la Bomba, Behind-the-Bakery, Carrer de l'Església, and the little square. No streams, because we'd sink; and the route is long enough as it is; if we tried it we'd never get it done, and besides it's really tiring. The rectory: the safe wall—okay? Now now, we don't need to cheat. Teresa stops—come on!—we run. It doesn't count: she was peeking. Teresa, kid, I already told you that you have to turn your back to us and face Santa Maria. If you do that then you don't have to close your eyes, but you can't move till we yell out. Let's see—do you guys understand me? Yeah, we'll take Carrer de la Torre; let's go over everything one more time. Not through the stream since the sand can trip you up. You're asking us to count again? We counted earlier, Teresa. That's not good enough? We're wasting time! It'll get dark, they'll bring the boats back in and we won't have even begun to play. What? The *Panxita* is coming back from Jamaica? That's no big deal. My father went further, all the way to Russia even. He came back with a fur coat and hair everywhere: he looked like a bear. My father always tells the story about when he went to give thanks to Friar Josep d'Alpens—who was on the pulpit—for the safe trip back, and he greeted my father with curses, like he was the devil. Come on, are we going to play or not? It's like yours was the only frigate in the world. Ai, kid, you're so stubborn! Let's count—and no complaining about whoever gets picked. *Macarrò, macarrò, xambà, xibirí, xibirí, mancà.* It's you again, little Teresa; that's tough. Everybody spread out! You're limping, Bareu? Wait up, guys. Bareu is limping. Does he get special rules or does he guard the area? Okay, then he helps keep an eye on it. Don't complain, little Teresa, you won't be doing the seeking by yourself. Come on. At last. Hey, facing the wall! Limping or not, if Bareu's the gatekeeper it's going to be impossible for us to get near the rectory. Who screamed "ready"? No, Teresa, no, we haven't hidden yet. Don't come down the stairs, little Teresa. I said don't come down the stairs—some good-for-nothing shouted out too early. Excuses? Me? A troublemaker? Me? Because I see I'm caught? You really don't want to play, do you! And you're mad that you have to stop, that's it. Don't come down the stairs, you hear me? Don't come down. Fine, get worked up about it. Sure, go ahead and run after me. I give up.»

# II

«You haven't seen them? Boy, where are you coming from? They've been back since yesterday! It was a noble three-month voyage this time, through the Baltic, then through Germany, Switzerland, Milan, Venice, and Florence—overland, of course. They left the *Panxita* in Danzig. It's strange—they didn't have to go to Italy. Their route was solely sea-bound: a commercial route. They must have persuaded the captain to change it to a pleasure trip, a romantic voyage. Their father gives them everything they ask him for. Today they're radiant, restrained and tireless. They brought back mountains of magnificent objects: glassware from Trieste, porcelain from Capodimonte, marbles, silks, medallions. They were seen in Fiesole with Vicenç de Pastor, or he went there to find them, because he loves Teresa. I suspect his return wasn't very triumphant: he's glum, his confidence has sunk. Yes, they're very pretty girls; and Teresa is more beautiful than Júlia, no? No, I don't buy that: Teresa is more beautiful. Above all, since they've returned I've noticed a splendor in her eyes, a distant light captured, a joy hidden and revealed at the same time. Júlia is more delicate. Her mother died of tuberculosis, keep that in mind, and that was a tremendous blow to the captain. I think he's in Trinidad now, surrounded by blacks and white trash. He married a Creole woman, perhaps she was even mixed; they have a wretched child—

a hunchbacked daughter—and I believe they're going through lean times. They're coming closer. Look how they come down the church's steps, barely brushing them. Teresa is exquisite—you can stick with Júlia. Go ahead and laugh about it, go ahead; but they look like duchesses. And this afternoon, at the arbor dance, they'll be queens.»

# III

«Don't greet Teresa. Don't greet her. She doesn't see anyone. How she's changed; she used to be so happy! It's that there've been so many blows, one after the other. After such slow agony, after fighting courageously for so many long months, Júlia died. The day after her death, the *Panxita* got stuck in the mouth of the Rhône. No, no, it won't be so great a financial loss, since Vallalta's rich; but he loved his frigate so much. Since it sank he's hated sailing and hasn't set out again. He just passes his days on his estate—the "Pietat"—contemplating the sea at a distance, surrounded by trees and books. He was so strong before, but now he is a dithering, decrepit old man. No more stories of sea adventures from him, he's lost his memory. What a man he was! They say that last century, in his younger days—thrill-seeker that he was back then—he even took part in Barceló's expedition against Algiers (although perhaps these stories don't add up), and after he was everywhere: Iloilo, Mexico, the Nicobar Islands, Newfoundland, Odessa; but now the captain wants nothing more than to die surrounded by the peace of his groves. His daughter looks after him, keeps an eye on him. Yes. Teresa is a woman of maybe forty years, maybe more, and Vicenç de Pastor is still waiting for word from her; but Teresa loves no one. Don't greet her, it's useless, she won't see you. She descends the stairs lifelessly.»

# IV

«Pay attention to how she descends the stairs. What a woman! Lady-like, slow, measured, and at the same time quick, at the pace no doubt of some practitioner's school, some lost style. Yes, Teresa is very old, you already know that; she's my age. Do I remember? We played together so often, right here in this square: tag, tic-tac-toe, planted soldier, leapfrog. All of that's way in the past now. The town seemed bigger to us back then—immense, richer in color and character. Running around we always discovered a hidden, new corner. Each afternoon, we waited in the sand for the boats to dock and the occasional return of some sailboat from America or China's remote seas. My father was a pilot, too, and he'd go as far as Russia, crossing frozen waters, skirting small glaciers. He'd return dressed in furs, like a bear; he scandalized the church with such luxury. Everything happened. One day, in the early evening, we plunged into the damp canebreak, chilled by the shiver of forbidden adventure. We groped our way forward, and it spun us round with the premonition of miracle. There was perhaps a cobweb of fog over Remei and a witches' storm-cloud at its heart, above the Muntala. And upon returning we told our grandparents about our run-in with a ghost. Everything happened. We grew up, and I married. Teresa and her sister Júlia, who died from tuberculosis years ago, traveled with Captain Vallalta in the *Panxita*. Later, the frigate sunk, and a little while afterward Júlia and the old man died. And there you have it. Teresa passes right by me without even a glance, with her hunchbacked niece—with her dog's shadow— behind her, she brushes up against me and doesn't even look, and my family is at least as old as hers, and I have to address her like I was an artisan. Everything happened. Teresa is a sad, old woman. She doesn't know how to laugh. And the town seems to me, and to her as well, I'm sure, so small, so empty and ramshackle! And way back when, we imagined it limitless, as if in a cloud. Carrer de la Bomba, Rera-la-fleca, Carrer de la Torre. Teresa used to come down the church steps so quickly. And now look at how she descends them. Still so ladylike, nevertheless—with a lady's step.»

# V

«You'll say, isn't the box of the "Frigata" made of good wood? And away she goes—the niece is stingy, come on now, but she wouldn't skimp one cent on a detail of such supposition. They carry the same blood from head to toe, and she won't expose herself to people's harsh tongues. Look, from caregiver, or worse, to executrix: the paths of life. Senyor Vicenç de Pastor is so hunched over! He looks like an axiom. Don't fool yourself, he's so old and so isolated, and they say he always loved her . . . who knows. Yes, quite a crowd; you don't see this sort of spectacle so often: women like the "Frigata" don't die every day. Uf, very rich—calculate it to be at least two hundred thousand gold pieces and you'd probably be short. All that money, all for the humpback. Ai, no, daughter, no, she's of no interest to me. God gave me a straight back and good health. I prefer that. Let's leave it at that! Look at how they surround her. Yesterday they were practically driving her off with the cracks of their whips; and today, look how they kiss up to her. Everyone is there: bouncy Bòtil, Coixa Fita, Caterina, Narcisa Mus. These last three ladies, all three of them, wrapped old "Frigata" in a shroud, because Paulina—the niece—wasn't capable of doing it, and they're already passing her the dish, the evil schemers. Do you know what Narcisa told me? Come here—while they were searching for her mantilla they found a box with some blond locks in it and the portrait of a man, the portrait of a young, tall, strong man. And, hold on, there was a name at the bottom; a strange Frenchie-sounding name. And no one ever suspected anything, given how much she traveled! And she was so hard, so proud. She wouldn't say hello to godmother—my godmother—because, God forgive her, she was poor; even though they played together as children. And now you see it: one, behind your back. Let's go. It's all just guessing. The thing is, maybe she never did anything wrong. Hush, they're bringing her down now. She must be heavy, and these stairs are narrow; I hope they don't slip. The wood is expensive, no doubt about it; it's expensive, I already told you that. The pallbearers are sweating, shameful, just look at the way they're sweating. Let's see if they crack it open at the bottom of the steps.»

# Psyche

«Slowly, the path of a hydrosol to a hydrogel or, if you'd prefer, the coagulation of a colloid. Or perhaps he died, he, the beloved, wretched body. Perhaps only the reflection of him on the waxy surface: conscience. And then I found myself—lost within an alien, difficult, bizarre geometrical realization. And I understood that I'd never influenced him. He had lived, and I, sacrificed to him from the beginning, indispensable ingredient, so that he could walk under the sun. And now again I've found myself—and my, have I found myself! I started, I started from I don't know where—light, idea—and I found, again, my form. Specifically: one, shall we say, very small butterfly; yes—that's it—a miniscule moth. With a voice. I can't place it inside, but rather more like all around, behind: I can't pinpoint it. I'm so young, I'm familiar with so little! I think of him, like him, so much still! I'm so scared of the black cat! . . . Come, come! . . . Radiant voice, at least. Inside, outside, and all around.

»I'm a moth: a small, a miniscule moth. Hands, paraffin? My voice, you know? And of "he," of "I." And now Pròspera has turned, perhaps because she heard him, and runs hastily toward the candles. The candles tremble under the demon's breath. The curtain of fire doesn't permit . . . doesn't permit the beast to pass. The cat keeps an eye on me, and moves, noisily, its paws. Don't blow out the flame! All I, him, stretched out, motionless, the belly swollen, juicy. Prior tasks . . . operation . . . to rot . . . Succulent. Pròspera contemplates him. How fat! Old, debaucherous woman, Pròspera. How she hates you, old man! Thirty years: always with Pròspera. And he kept his eyes fixed on her, as a hobby, to—how can I put it—to scare her . . . a little. But he failed, because Pròspera knows that his company won't be solicited, that she can't touch. She stayed up with him, snoring, the greedy beast kept an eye on him. The candles burn so high! . . .The mirror, covered . . . And then I found my way in the darkness and slipped through its half-opened mouth. The closest candle drew me in. The candle . . . it swept away the visible breaths. And I should have freed myself from the dominion of the gluttonous pawed beast. Paws! . . . I'm so scared of the black cat!

»But the candles shone high, magnificent candles, and they cleared my path. I saw myself, I saw it. Moth, body? It suffered so much, I suffered so much! Lean, skeletal, a coagulated colloid: that's all. All? Who will redeem the vulgarity of things? . . . Pròspera. How ugly! Real. Without secrets, infinitesimally localized. Don't snore. Don't make any noise. I'm a moth. A miserable, minuscule moth. I want to get outside, out of the darkness. Make no noise. It hurts. I'm a moth. A voice. A thought tied to instincts. An ex-life. Pròspera snores, and her panting distances the gloomy path, the cat spies the path of gloom. But the candles are so high!

And I so love this body, I love it so! I cannot abandon the circle of fire, the rotten circle, the ex-life. I cannot, because they see me, you know? I swell. If I were smaller. If I were invisible . . . But they see me. He was generous, he was being vain, and I, for these characteristics, am condemned to be seen. A great moth: I swell.

»Pròspera awakens. Wake up, Pròspera! How ugly, how old, how yellow! She awakens, prays. But are you thinking, Pròspera, about money, about some bad stew, about stews, about the bed? She's sleepy, it's natural. He didn't love her—that said, she looked after him, out of custom is how I'd put it to you all. Out of loyalty to that image, so ancient, of thirty years ago. You and me, him, Pròspera, thirty years ago. The mirror, covered. Pròspera is dry, lacks imagination. Just, just the custom, a ring, some words, a buzz, an echo. That's all.

»Pròspera yawns. She's tired. She looks and looks again at the bed, she prays. She fell asleep lightly thinking of the white sheets, of the money. He rotted away unnoticed. The beast, a glutton, spied. The candles burned. I think in circles. How am I going to slip out toward the darkness without falling to the empire of the cat? Ai, ai, ai. Pròspera has seen me. What is that? A moth, a moth, a moth, Pròspera! Ai, ai, ai, you trap me, you gather me in your hands! Will this, perhaps, be the way? The way towards the darkness, far from the beast, from the candles, from Pròspera, from the voice, from the ex-life, toward that morsel of God . . . eh! . . . that which is my share.«

Suddenly, a clean hit: the common sound of one palm against the other. The voice stopped, a painting fell noisily from the wall, the hour chimed, someone turned on the lights, two of them, fervently faithful, had had an accident. «The stage machinery worked tonight for Saurimonda,» applauded young Estengre. «As I've understood it, this Pròspera knows where she has her right hand and her left, and that's it,» Uncle Nicolau Mutsu-Hito approvingly said. «And she doesn't stand for moths eating holes in her clothes. I'm smashing any moths that come within reach too,» assured Senyora Magdalena Blasi.

# Nebuchadnezzar

*To Justi Petri, Arcadian of Rome, studious, in process,
from biblio-babylonic problems.*

## I

His father's side of the family were people of the earth, like all of
you, like me, like all of the citizens of Konilòsia. As for his mother's side, they returned to the earth. Nebuchadnezzar Puig was
his name. He inherited the «Puig» from his father. The «Nebuchadnezzar» from the devout affection directed at him by his
great-grandmother, a pious Englishwoman. The pious branch of
the family had fallen into an abundant current of Catholicism,
and amidst this fervor arrived Nebuchadnezzar, a man of good
sense, steeped in positive indifference, whose holding pattern
held until his good death. The war of '14 found him working as a
cobbler—and he made a living out of it. That story flew over his

head, neither enriching him nor, for that matter, refining him, and Nebuchadnezzar failed to take advantage of the unique opportunity before him to be heard merely for the sake of the money he made, as would a man of culture and pedigree. Like those of his town, he had, however, good sense. He possessed concrete ideas about life, love, and changes of weather—and he made a living out of it. Touching upon love, he was always partial toward making it legal through marriage—any affirmation to the contrary is inaccurate—but he didn't give getting it right much of a chance. It frightened Nebuchadnezzar to see his friends embark on that adventure so easily.

«When I do it! Don't rush me. Yeah, look at him! After, to the gallows and crack! A laughing stock, right? Me, dangling, hunted down, no doubt. No way, don't complicate things for me. When will I be better off than I am now?»

It was true. Nebuchadnezzar was happy, he prospered before the Lord and scoffed at pointed questions. And everyone envied him and hailed his perspicacity. And he was taken for a fearsome man, a man of experience.

«No, certainly not, they fool you. They're not going to snare me.»

Until he ran into Evangelina. And they wed.

# II

Six months later, Evangelina gave birth to a daughter. And all in Nebuchadnezzar's spirit was desolation. And he cried and promised a bloodbath, an exemplary vengeance. And he did nothing. He thought it over calmly, requested censure of opinion, and found out whose the child was; it turned out the father was a powerful man. Nebuchadnezzar accepted the requisite smearing and took the child to be baptized. Was it permissible to decide to do anything else to innocent flesh? The flesh was redeemed by gold or holy water. They gave her the name «Candelera.»

The truth, however, instantly made its way around the humid, dirty town with its worn-down geometry of doors and sunless windows. And Nebuchadnezzar was the laughing stock of his neighbors who had, until yesterday, admired him. He saddened, quit his job, and started going to the bar. And, already a professional drunk by this point, he took to screaming at all and sundry his ignominy: that he had lost his cool and his glory, his famous perspicacity. That he no longer earned an honorable living.

«They bought me. I'm a bought man and I say nothing. That's why I didn't throw them out of my house. They pay me.»

They called him, for the likeness, "Widow Belly." A Plautian yelled out to him:

«You're lost. You don't deserve the name "Nebuchadnezzar." It's too long. I'm going to call you just "Neb." I'll save some spit. Crisis, boy.»

He assented, filled with sadness:

«Yes, I am lost. Call me "Neb."»

Work complete. Justice done. Degradation. He already is, and always will be, Neb Widow Belly; or, shorter still, Neb.

# III

Senyor Pepa Sastre, potentate, expanded the Neb family with two more members: Oliva and Perpètua. Males weren't born of that happy union, and so Senyor Pepa Sastre, who wanted an heir, tired in the long run of maintaining Evangelina and her unsatisfactory lineage and withdrew almost all of his financial assistance. He was a refined and sentimental man. A man in possession of these qualities never goes as far as to completely break old ties. From a distance Senyor Pepa Sastre kept an eye on the physical and ethical upbringing (Evangelina had turned decadent and flabby) of the three little girls, which was guided along the right path by good Neb, whom they gratefully loved like a father. After knowing their choice, Senyor Pepa Sastre could only sigh. «They're doing well,» he said meditatively. «They are young, pretty, strong. May they gosh darn get to work!» Senyor Pepa Sastre, ever the patriot, was a solidly doctrinaire and sufficiently rigorous liberal.

Meanwhile, Neb was getting older. Everything was ending for him in this life. God, who chokes but doesn't exactly strangle, had pity on the guy. Neb was slightly redeemed from the little thing still dragging on the ground—from Senyor Pepa Sastre's desertion—by the effort of his lucrative daughters. He had been prudent and now he could pass entire days at the bar. The old conjugal wound somehow managed to heal and, as tends to happen with old stories, it acquired prestige in the eyes of the younger generations (may the illustrious Petri take note that the war of '14 did not ennoble poor Neb). His daughters would hurry about under his orders, and he was an expert in talking about it.

«May they always be good with money, praised be God.»

«They always are,» affirmed a meddler.

«Naturally. They tuck away coins, and so, God willing, they will be able to retire.»

Ecolampadi Miravitlles, a reformer riddled with quixotism, who visited all three girls and made no distinction among them, opined:

«Sibling love can sour an affair.»

«It is life's path,» said Xanna the coachman, philosophically.

But, passing through, he said it in a language so dense that no one understood him.

# IV

And Neb followed his life's path in its entirety and arrived at the end. And he was cried for by Evangelina and watched over by Candelera, Oliva, and Perpètua, who took some days off to care for Neb. And, in dying, the tears of Pasquala Estampa, Cristeta Mils, and Pudentil·la Closa, neighbors, fell around him, and those, too, of Doloretes Bòtil, wing-wounded, so bouncy, and the sniffles of Esperanceta Trinquis, who was like a sister to him. And, in that supreme moment, the aides of Father Silví Saperes would not fail to be accounted for. His soul was freed, then, to its Creator. Comforted by religion, and by the praise of those who'd loved and respected him in life: everyone who'd dealt with him. And he was, upon leaving the valley, sixty-two years, three months, and a day or so old. And, now dead, they fit him in a coffin.

«He ended up so small,» observed Senyor Pepa Sastre, who had come expressly to see him. «He was nothing but Neb from head to toe,» he declared, his emotion poorly hid.

«Don't take him away yet!» Evangelina cried out. Candelera, Oliva, and Perpètua wept.

Sirac's son Jesús said: «Do not return good to those who have done bad to you. Consider . . .» But why remind you of the greatest, sublime, illustrious Roman academic. Having returned that day—out of respect—to extend Nebuchadnezzar a baptism, they left him cold inside his coffin, with the moaning of widow and children, those virtuous women, all around him. And the body was towed by a skeletal horse out of the tattered geometry of the suburb and buried under the dirt of a cypress. And Father Silví Saperes intoned with reverence a prayer for the eternal rest of his soul. And opulent Senyor Pepa Sastre, who presided over the act—by his own choice—delivered an ennobling speech in memory of the deceased. And that is how the great Nebuchadnezzar, cobbler and drunk, found peace with the ritual. And after, everyone left. And these were their final comments:

«The soil is soft and there isn't much thickness to it. They shouldn't touch it.»

Everyone laughed.

«An institution has disappeared,» summed up Father Silví, resuscitator of the archival glories of the suburb.

«And now, off to work, girls,» Evangelina advised Candelera, Oliva, and Perpètua.

And these were the funeral rites of Nebuchadnezzar.

# V

«Vulgar,» Pupú Alosa, the reader, said, rejecting the story. «Does it not seem vulgar to you?» she asked Ludovicus Baronet, with an enchanting smile.

«Yes, dear, vulgar,» confirmed the exquisite L.B.

«Oh, very vulgar,» ratified the authority Pulcre Trompel·li, with her tottering hump.

«Too vulgar»—who knows if this was the thought of Justi Petri, Arcadian of the Roman Academy.

«Yes, illustrious academic, select public, ladies and gentleman,» agreed the ventriloquist Salom, welcomingly. «Extremely vulgar, it is true, really extremely vulgar. *Et pourquoi pas?*»

# Death in the Street

«That's not it,» said the Cervantist, directing himself toward Efrem Pedagog, who was right next to him. «That's not it, I tell you,» he insisted, congested. «The book explains it clearly: Altisidora saw a dozen demons at the gates of hell. Silence! I know what you all mean: the man doesn't have enough substance to coax out so many demons. But why choose Altisidora? He could have named the heroine of the farce, let's say for the sake of discussion, "Cristòfora," and not sullied the memory of the maiden.» «What's in it!» contradicted Ecolampadi Miravitlles, who had approached them in the meantime. «Is it your precious scholarly memory that gets to demand who makes a living? Whether Altisidora or Cristòfora, the spectacle has stopped us in our tracks, captured our attention in the middle of the street, under the sun.» «It's burning hot out here,» intervened the amusing Senyora Magdalena Blasi, passionate for climatology. «Good day, it's true, and with all the rain yesterday this was by no means a given. It's glorious to live here, glorious.» «One of our unique glories, dear madam,» Efrem Pedagog said. «Well,» he continued. «We were arguing, gentlemen, over the veracity of the farce represented before us. I cannot confirm (the pace of my life prohibits me from having the scholarly data at hand) the exact name of the demons that Altisidora saw on her feigned voyage to the underworld.» «A dozen, my good man!» erupted the Cervantist. «Perhaps you doubt it, sir? I am willing to wager . . . » «Let us leave it at that,» conceded Efrem Pedagog. «I believe you, sir. But that is not of importance. External, historical truth only, my good man.» «Agreed,» agreed Ecolampadi Miravitlles. «The internal is the important truth, and you can by no means deny that this, despite its imperfections, does not meld with the spectacle we are witnessing.» «Oh, oh!» said Efrem Pedagog, posing, a little bothered by the interruption, his eyes blank. «Note the way art—barbaric and luminous—knew just how to discover the psychological refinement within the fable. The maiden mocked love and deserved hell, a vulgar hell of puppets, cardboard, stage backdrops. Altisidora is pretty. She does not have, however, a noble soul. She is exquisite and unreachable because that was what made her an example of quixotic chastity, not for her own sake. I fear, gentlemen, that Altisidora will not be revived here. Here we will witness the ultra-earthly luck of dead Altisidora, truly dead, without resurrections, just as the Catholic and popular mind imagines her. Altisidora . . . » «The things you know, sir!» Senyora Magdalena Blasi, staring at him, said. «But, did you say Catholic? For the love of God, don't speak of religion now. I'm so fragile!» «Be quiet!» Estanislau Forns, a young technician employed by the grocery store and a member of the «Conscious and Totalitarian Sporting Youths of Town,» demanded rather rudely.

«What do you mean, speaking to a lady in this manner?» cried out the unconquered hybrid General Don Bartolomé Morros de los Cabezos. «Out of my sight, lest I teach you a lesson for your impudence!» «Thank you!» the old woman with the fine mouth said to that genuine national treasure. «One is exposed to so many things these days!» The General gestured gallantly. And behold how (with Efrem still savoring the lady's compliment) Altisidora and the demon—who had been, until then, so arrogant on the small fair-and-street-corner puppet stage—tottered, fell silent, and vanished, tumbling down toward hell's invisible circles. «What's going on?» asked the large and honorable crowd. It was one in the afternoon. «Is it snack time?» the crowd wondered, and began to prepare for an orderly exit. «What's wrong with this guy?» a small woman with a heavy chest, Pura Yerovi, cried out, having practically stopped in her tracks. «It's coming down!» The little portable stage fell. Under the ruins, a body, its hands still gloved with Altisidora and the demon. «A doctor!» demanded various voices. «Are you a doctor? What's wrong with this guy?» «He's dead,» the practitioner said with certainty. «How?» asked the crowd. «Who can be sure, who knows,» he answered indifferently. «And now, dead! It's strange, under this sky,» opined heavy-chested Pura Yerovi. At that moment, a disheveled boy yelled out that he was a relative and leapt on top of the dead man. «Poor kid, this is so beautiful,» said Senyora Magdalena Blasi. «Police!» roared the heroic General. «Someone call the police! There is no way this can be happening.» «You are correct, this is a cabal,» Efrem Pedagog said dismissively. «Dying in this manner, on the street, without even the most basic public service yet in motion. And, well, what were we saying—Altisidora . . . » «Psychological explanations get me nowhere. A dozen demons: this is the honest truth. I do not know the malevolent intention behind it, be it intentional, external, scholarly. External? I prefer that,» the irascible Cervantist categorically decided. «I agree with the other gentleman,» confessed Ecolampadi Miravitlles. And off they went. «Are the police not on their way?» insisted, still, the General. «The unhappy thing, an abandoned boy, how miserable! I'm going to fall ill,» young Pura Yerovi said, everything emanating from her heavy chest. «What a glorious sunny day,» murmured Senyora Magdalena Blasi, as she was lost amid the growing multitude. «Life, what a trip. Since you entertained me, poor thing, I'll say the Lord's Prayer for you. They were wise, those gentlemen. And wow, how hungry I've become,» realized, impartially, Senyora Magdalena Blasi.

# German Quasi-Story of Ulrika Thöus

On a celebrated occasion many years ago, my friend Frau Doktor Ulrika Thöus, of the Institut für Vererbungsforschung of the College of Architecture in Berlin-Dahlem, wrote me a letter in German that I translated, via the delicate fogginess known as «public refinement,» into my moribund imperial tongue. «You know,» my illustrious lady friend said, «the work of R. Goldschmidt's team, *Die sexuellen Zwischenstufen*, and the works of Meisenheimer, Harrison, and of my colleague Pariser. I suspect you know as well the studies done by Witschi on certain geographic races of frogs, and I assume you accept without discussion the rigor of Mendel's laws as they pertain to the inheritance of sexes. It explains to us that, in beings of separate sexes, one sex forms, generally, in the animal kingdom as well as in that of the plants, two classes of gametes (X, Y), which is to say that it is heterogametic. In turn, the other sex is homogametic (X, X). What consequences would you draw from within the range of Goldschmidt's extensive studies of intersex before a deviation of the numerical relation of the Mendel inheritance of 1:1 or, if you would like it in the more commonly understood terms, 50% ♂♂ 50% ♀♀? I have experimented with numerous combinations of distinct species of the genus "Triton." A microscopic examination of one hundred and twenty-three gonads revealed twenty-one cases in which ovaries developed, one in which a single testicle developed. And the remaining organism, more or less "a speck," had an undifferentiated gonad in the middle of many ovaries. It is a strange result, do you not think? This is indisputable evidence that what we are talking about here are true hybrids: look, if you will, at the photograph I have included for you. You will distinguish in it four species, all of them represented in Germany, four of that country's species of "Triton": the "vularis," the "cristatus," the "alpestris," and the "palmatus." I crossed them in the following manner: vulgaris x cristatus, vulgaris x palmatus, palmatus x vulgaris, vulgaris x alpestris, palmatus x cristatus (it should be noted that the female always comes first). And I observed this percentage. What could be the cause of this predominance of ovaries? Goldschmidt would have explained it as being due to the transformation of all of the males into females, but this is not viable. 100% ♀. Imagine! And do not offer me, I beg you, Federley's affirmation of the chromatic combinations in the Lepidoptera.»

Having arrived at this point, Doktor Ulrika Thöus, a little excited, disserted largely about the theory of Federley, the Finn. Ulrika didn't like the Finnish—perhaps because of the remote Ural-Altaic origins of that nation—and for a while this dislike came out in an absolutely anti-Mendelian tone. But the beloved Aryan friend found her way back to scientific equanimity and began again to discuss the ever-important matter of the deviation of the numerical relation between the sexes as they pertained to the genus of salamander under discussion. «Nevertheless, whatever the case may be regarding the Finn, I firmly believe in Federley's affirmations,» conceded Ulrika. «Read those in "Heredities," XII, 1929. —*Über subletale und disharmonische Chromosomen-kombinationen*. Are you familiar with these? Perhaps you are not in agreement with them? Have you investigated some fact, unknown to us, prior or posterior to the fertilization, which may be able to impede the development of the masculine sex, which may explain the appearance of a testicle (just one, mind) among so many ovaries? If you have, let me know immediately; I await the judgment of the master. Regarding my position on the matter, I can guarantee that my experiments corroborate those of the wise Finn concerning the Lepidoptera. All the $\male\male$ convert into $\female\female$, because the Y chromosome (I allude to Federley) is too weak to overcome the energetic action of the X and determine the emergence of the testicles. If you have another criterion, write to me. I know you are skeptical about "Triton," but no matter. Yours, Dr. Ulrika Thöus.»

Back then I thought, genius that I was, that what Ulrika claimed couldn't be so. I answered her right away, and my response went as follows:

«Frau Doktor Ulrika Thöus. Institut für Vererbungsforschung. Berlin-Dahlem. —If, as you have informed me, my distinguished friend, one lone testicle and one that doesn't count as a testicle end up together amid so many ovaries as vulgaris x cristatus, vulgaris x palmatus, palmatus x vulgaris, vulgaris x alpestris, and palmatus x cristatus, I am convinced that your conclusions arise from an overwhelming pessimism. But without question, apart from the neatness and competence for which they are well known, there absolutely must be some lamentable error in your observations. Some testicles were probably disguised as ovaries before your very eyes, which were likely fatigued: this is excusable. Look for them, then, beloved friend, and do not doubt that you will find them. For hidden though they may be—and it is incontrovertible that they are—sooner or later the testicles will have to appear. Eagerly awaiting the good news, it gives me pleasure in the meantime to offer myself to you for anything you may need in your exhausting research on the sexes.»

# Nerves

That afternoon Salom had seen *M*, a German film about as unpleasant as Konilòsia and Alfaranja on the lips of Lavínia's devoted bourgeoisie. It was the story of the vampire of Düsseldorf. The tragedy of that lymphatic monster left Salom, as he confessed to himself, impressed. He left the cinema unsettled, in a rush, without the desire even to lift his head; he didn't have a handle on his nerves. Did something sinister threaten him that night? Hell, the sky was filled with stars and the wind rocked a fat moon. The moon chilled him. The clear, metallic moon. He walked through already well-deserted streets. A vagabond crossed his path. He was a thin and ambiguous man. His left arm was cut off above the elbow: he showed off the piece of it remaining to the prying air.

«For the love of God, a bit of charity.»

Salom picked up his pace.

«God will take it into account.»

He ran, calling after Salom:

«A bit of charity!»

«Go away, brother, I'm not carrying any cash on me,» Salom said to him. The other man did not respond. He limited himself to bringing his mutilated arm closer to Salom's face, closer to his skin. A deep whiff of neglect, lust, and pus rose up his nose.

«Well, what do you want from me?» Salom asked him. The other continued generously revealing to him the secrets of his flesh. Salom, growing curious, allowed him. The man began to sweat and turn pale. The moral of his complex business lost, he screamed.

«What nerve, you make me sick! What, don't you have any guts *or* any decency?»

«Only a smidgeon of disgust,» Salom, pronouncing his words neatly, said; because it was true and because he was defending, among other things, his property.

The stench receded, and Salom, satisfied with his behavior, smiled. If he saved some principle and his money, the rest was basically empty words, sentimentalism. What had happened had toned his nerves, and he was already devoting himself to optimistic dreams when, from behind, an unknown began to whistle a tune. Salom recognized the notes. Yes, he had heard them not too long ago in the cinema: the whistling of the vampire, of the *Kindermörder*. His blood iced over. The whistling grew closer. It rang in his ear. Salom closed his eyes. The neck, his neck, murderer! A young man passed, innocent and pacific. Why did such a ridiculous terror overcome Salom? His nerves, he lacked nerve. He went on with his life. A soldier and a girl embraced and kissed each other delightedly on a corner. Salom smiled again, understanding. Yes, it was already so now: this girl had already run into her *Kindermörder*. But what did it say? Where was it? The street, deserted.

The stones, humid. The asphalt, gleaming like a mirror. Behind a mound of trash, under a tremulous and very weak streetlight, a black cat twirled its whiskers and scraped clean the skeleton of a herring. The tail cleaned the municipal slabs of waste particles. It was a wise cat, with an insolent stare, and its attitude offended Salom. Little by little, practically on tiptoe, with the available foot . . . The cat guessed it. The herring fell from its snout and tumbled to the asphalt with the trash. Salom's foot fell back to its normal position, and his voice sweetened, full of flattery, but the cat's kittens spied Salom fixedly, as though he were a herring, and he could read in that moment a firm and meditated ill will. He fled from it. Then the last old-style seller of newspapers yelled out, full-voiced, the day's goods. Corruption; shoddiness; violence; wars; crimes; social ills; sky-high inflation; manipulated statistics; snide triumphalism; conspiratorial, anti-establishmentarian social climbing; vacuous, unencumbered freedom of speech. The same as always.

«Thief, thief, grab him!»

Uproar from a porter's lodge. Expectation. Some police came down that building's stairway carrying, detained, an extremely frightened albino boy of about nineteen years old. A country bumpkin asked:

«'Scuse me. Has someone died?»

Upon hearing this the woman-who-usually-takes-care-of-the-entrance let out a hysterical yell:

«Worse: he stole thirty *sagrades* from me. He broke into my dresser drawer.»

Everyone felt sorry for her:

«Poor Secundina! Poor Secundina Llopart!»

They calmed her:

«Enough, enough, they already got it back. Poor thing, it's the jolt. I'll take care of it. Would you like some lime blossom tea, Secundineta?»

Salom separated himself from the group of neighbors and finally arrived home. He was affected, feverish. «These nerves,» he said to himself. «Perhaps I will have to start to concern myself with this in earnest. Will something worrisome have to happen to me? My nerves, imbalance, too much work, perhaps. I'll have to rest for a while.»

«Where would you most like to travel to?» he asked his only love, the woman of his life. «I must rest: *surmenage*, my nerves, etc.»

«I have no clothes!» she responded, her pupils wide. «A trip? You're so kind, so generous! I'll have to make six or eight dresses and I already have the kinds picked out, they're marvelous. And we can go to Hawaii and also to Venice, if that sounds good to you. Aren't you happy? You don't love me! Ah, ten dresses, don't say no. You feel beat down by your nerves . . . Yes, it's typical. Why are you so quiet? You don't like what I'm wearing? Something cheaper! . . . Hawaii, Venice . . . But are you nervous or really sick? Don't get me all worried!» she, his only love, the woman of his life, said to Salom, to Salom's immense fatigue. And in that particular, insignificant cell within which the universe presides adrift, Salom was a deflated culprit, with neither relief for his sorrow nor hope for a pardon, another convict among others, among other hundreds of millions, under the jurisdiction of the trivial stupidities of affection, of style, and of death.

# The Rise and Fall of Esperança Trinquis

# I

«Trinquis, Trinquis!»

A *sardana*[1] and mockery round about the drunk woman.

«Trinquis, Trinquis!»

The children, not sufficiently satisfied with their screaming, took to their slingshots. One rock sported the tarot of the beggar. Esperanceta Trinquis (inflated nose, slumped stockings, honestly not too sharp) discovered with her doughy tongue:

«Is this a system to establish follow-up lectures?»

The children stopped, because a pause in the dialogue was always a drag and no action makes sense without commentary and the luster of the word. They observed a profound cyclic law (vicious needn't be said) with the ignorance of kids and the unfortunate. They yelled from afar and feigned being afraid. Bassot spoke for everyone:

---

1   A traditional Catalan dance performed by group in a circle. –RrP

«Don't you see that you're drunk? Who, if they're not drunk, can penetrate the muddle of what you're saying?»

They laughed. Trinquis countered:

«The reasons for my *mui*[2] are obvious, despite some shameless opinions here. On the other hand, whether I'm here or not here, the lady basically revolts all of you?»

Bassot responded, making a great fuss:

«Don't even think it, Trinquis. There isn't even the hint of a grudge on our part. Isn't your booze—stuff as good to you as any prestige—better than everything else you imagined? Where do you hide the habit? It's always been done this way, and you do it pretty well, you're no pushover. If you were, those bones would be dancing.»

He pointed to the mountain Mal Temps and the cemetery, the borders of Sinera.

«Fine, go on, laugh,» said Trinquis. «Now, just don't hurt me, okay?»

«The taunting never gets out of hand,» Bassot said. «Hey, boys, let's go!»

«Wait!» Trinquis said. «I am, it's true, predisposed to fighting. But do you know who you're exchanging ideas with? A lady, ep!, a lady. These plushies led Neb to his last lather, consider that!»

«Neb of which book?» asked Bassot. «You're delivering sacraments like a troublemaker, Trinquis.»

«Hardly,» she asserted. «That's enough, grandchildren. Hey, writer, take me away from the buzzing of this swarm!» she yelled

---

2  "Mouth" in Caló, commonly referred to as the language of gypsies, a mixed Romani and Romance language. –RrP

out to me. «Don't make me come off like I'm getting even more plastered.»

«If you are, what can we do about it,» I said. «History says that we have to throw stones at you now. Come on, lady, don't fight it, it's useless. I'm staying out of it.»

«*Quin deu*!» blasphemed Trinquis.

«Pirandellian![3]» I responded, rancorously.

«Come on, that's enough—so many *sorabis*[4] here »

«Break open the five bottles of ratafia, angels!»

# II

«Since you're in control of it, I can't deny our relation,» the old woman said to me biliously. «I hate you, you know. Thanks to you, Bassot made me, of course, abandon my protector, and the muddle in me cleared up from top to bottom. And you should have been able to make my destiny easier to manage, and you refused. However, I'm your character and I'm obsessed with you. Well, then: my story, all larded up. I don't know why you're chasing my shadow after so many years way off in the distance. Melera's life-long friend. To roll by, slap, and that's it. A little drink now and again. Yeah, to forget things, Jesus. And all of a sud-

---

3   As in Luigi Pirandello (1867-1936), Italian dramatist, novelist, and short-story writer. −RrP

4   Possibly in reference to "la professor indígena" Aurembiaix Sorabis from another of Espriu's prose works, *Les roques i el mar, el blau*. Espriu's characters reappear frequently in his various works of poetry and prose. −RrP

den you're here exploiting my fame, and I didn't take any more swigs than Melera or Neb, I swear. With that one: like siblings. I watched him die.»

«Is it true that Candelera, Oliva, and Perpètua were all there?» I asked with the anxiousness of an evangelist.

«Yes. The widow, Pepa Sastre, Pasquala Estampa, Pudentil·la Closa, Criseta Mils, and Doloretes Bòtil, too. The whole family. What a moment! We cried. Death was slow in coming. We told little stories to entertain ourselves. Death saw all of us off with sacraments and resignations. Father Silví led the Our Father. Death, however, was slow in arriving. So we formed a circle and we kept an eye on him until things sped up. We cried, with our eyes fixed on him, bet your life. Spectacle, child. The street grew gloomy in the long run, and we were to the point where we didn't see him in really bad shape. We're talking about the end of September! We distracted ourselves for a few instants, because things there were going slowly; we meddled with our hair. Until she, she was the nearest (it was her turn, the poor girl), said: "That's it!" We breathed.»

«That was how Nebuchadnezzar died?» I said.

«Didn't I just tell you so? Evangelized,» Trinquis, cutting in, said. «And I haven't been able to erase it from my mind ever since.»

«Glory is in the persistence of memory,» I offered.

«What?,» Trinquis said.

«Nothing,» I murmured. «And tell me: this was the most exalted moment of your life?»

«If you say so, what choice do I have!,» Trinquis answered. «Anyway, it was an illustrious feeling of courteous behavior. Hey, it's over,» she added. «You have no further right to my conversation, child. I'm leaving.»

«Trinquis!,» I called out to her.

But she was already gone.

# III

«Yes,» Bassot said to me. «You weren't born yet. I don't know why that waste interests you so much. As little kids, we chased her, throwing stones. It's what's done. She went from one place to another all frayed. She got drunk a lot. She sang "en un taller," etc. She was very popular. Until Melera, the queen of caves, supplanted her. Imagine! And suddenly, she disappeared. One snowy day, she fell through a hole, a low point, on the train's tracks. She'd walk around covered in sulfur. The snow got to her, and the next day we found her a breath away from the rancid wine, cold.»

«And was it sunny that day?» I asked, distressed.

«Which? The day after it snowed? Glorious weather; fitting for these countries. Why are you thinking of that now?»

# First and Only Run-In with Zaraat

«It is neither mockery nor pedantry. Above all, it is not pedantry,» assured the sensitive and cultured Miravitlles. «I do not know Hebrew either, and I hope that this unknown word does not frighten us: that is all I seek. How your indifferent laughter would freeze if you all knew it! However, in order to tell you the story of my run-in with Zaraat, I am counting on your ignorance as a strong ally.»

«Ugh!» voices protested.

The narrator continued:

«A curious, stimulated person, were they to hurriedly consult any dictionary, would say, trembling: "Zaraat in this day and age? Lie. We do not pay heed to medieval fantasies." There are specters so distant from, so foreign to our lives, that we arrive at morbid extremes in our desire to have contact with them, with their impossible presence. I, I myself forever longed to encounter Zaraat; I felt fascinated by his legend. Zaraat now suddenly spoke to me, through the mouth of that woman. Zaraat the banished, the ancient, the reviled, who delighted in infinite putrefactions. Yes, latent then as well: Zaraat, a step away. The ravenous Zaraat, one step away, waiting to pounce on me from the mouth of a miserable woman, and, wracked with agony from wanting to evade her, I cried out for help in the form of a feeble and useless science of pots and jars. Naked horror before the mirror that was Zaraat, where she celebrated, eyeing me the entire time. There is no emotion more steeped in the broth of literary ruins, I tell you, than my run-in with Zaraat. Strong, brutal, clear poetry. Zaraat, present there, and me before her, still, alone, abandoned, and good. Secundina Llopart, present there without making sense of its meaning, effusively, corporeally pitying, the luckless woman. She stopped her, kissed her, she did not know that she was speaking with Zaraat. How far away the Middle Ages, how far away the choice blasphemies of Joinville,[5] pardoned by a saint, a selection that our poorly-plugged, dainty, anemone-like ears cannot hear. Zaraat with everything, a step away; exit without motive, without logic. Strong, unashamed of her putrefaction in the glaciered sunlight.»

«New Cicero,» went the snide, admiring murmurs.

The orator continued:

«And, of course, before me the victim, a woman with a voice still beautiful, who Zaraat felt the need to respect. A poor, hard-working woman, mother of many small children. It was already a heavily burdensome process, and she, fooled, knew nothing about it until the end. The woman relived her long days of misery, count-

---

5    Jean de Joinville (1224–1317): French writer and chronicler.

ing them and arriving at no end: a burden and a societal travesty, with one exception to my benefit: I can bring her to the attention of all of you. Sad, tearful, the woman ignored her link with Zaraat. Secundina Llopart consoled her effusively, physically. If only she were to have translated the name! The secret, so close to tumbling from the throat: count, here, Zaraat. What a leap Secundina would have taken! What would she have made with her effusive, physical, noisy compassion? The scream, a mouth, Zaraat. But also lonely, unfortunate, tearful, sad, human.»

«So, you didn't reveal the secret?» someone asked.

«No, I preferred to extend a hand to Zaraat,» responded Miravitlles. «I extended a hand to her even though I remembered the words of Joinville. Heroism, self-control, literature? Whatever it is that is wanted, may it serve me, "while the hour to praise Santa Maria comes to me," to even out the balance of so very many shortcomings. Meanwhile, I did not stop washing myself for two days, until I began to chafe, the palm of my hand infected.»

«Of course, the soap!» pondered a few of the unconditionally conscientious.

«You exaggerate, you dramatize,» Doctor Robuster i Tramusset—licensed only in medicine and introduced unexpectedly—said, letting the air out of the room. «The danger of contagion from the authentic Zaraat (because you can't forget that it is a rather imprecise and ambiguous word and, moreover, rather difficult to transcribe with adequate diacritics) has been during all epochs very relative. On the other hand, you can certainly believe it to be a problem now practically solved. With diaminodiphenylsulfone or any equivalent substance. The medication must be ordered, as is notoriously the case, with extreme prudence.»

«And it is administered if there are sharp reactions, or, in isolated cases, corticoids,» answered the modest and encyclopedic Miravitlles. «I give it to you that the latest techniques have entirely changed the subject. But my anecdote is from quite a few years ago, though it would be no pleasure to be cornered by Zaraat even today,» he added with model level-headedness, as the entertainingly vengeful and ignorant debaters, all laboratory propaganda shut out of the honorable and short controversy, realized with cruel clarity that the developing story had ended on the tail of a fish.

# Magnolias in the Cloister

*Revised, to Joan Triadú.*

«You're in the cloister,» I said to my skeleton, «and you're not saluting the presence and the miracle of the magnolias?» «Lyrics now? I'm tired, sit down,» my skeleton commanded. «Not even you can free me from impending death?» I queried the trees. «Must I always feel a slave to these abominable bones?» «Ai, poor, poor us!» responded the flowering magnolias. «We can't help you, a curse bewitches us, we dare not move. Don't you see how the young palm envies us?» And they shook their ultra-green foliage as proof of their useless tenderness. «The young palm doesn't like me,» I said. «It will never fail to reach the bell tower and the old bells. You would end up missing those peaks tremendously,» I said to the yellow palm. «I don't know why you insist upon continuing bowed in the stifling cloister. Every morning, at dawn, the swallows dispatch to the old mothers a desert welcome, one from far-off shadows, the cry of prayer to distant minarets. Wouldn't it please you to hear it, wouldn't it appeal to you?» But the palm was silent and spied with great spite the beauty of the magnolias. Meanwhile, the sun had spread out over the slabs of the cloister, and the gothic cobwebs of the altars remained in the dark. The paintbrush of gold extended its offering back above the chill of the sculptures. «You, with the spell on the immobilized magnolias,» I then yelled at the palm, «you could have at least told me how to free myself from my carcass.» «Ask the water,» the palm suddenly yelled back at me. «I'm just looking at the magnolias. I've been looking at them for years, absorbing, little by little, their beauty, but I haven't sapped them dry yet, and I'm ignoring whether it will allow me in the end to proclaim that I am beautiful. Tell me that I am,» commanded the palm. «Talk to my bones,» I responded as I went toward the fountain and the geese's sink. The peacefulness of water trickled from the fountain. «This water was just born and probably doesn't know the secret,» I thought. «I'll go ask the settling surface of the geese's sink. I'd quarreled,» I said, «with my skeleton, this, my unbearable guest. I live enslaved by him, as unknown as he is intimate. How did we end up linked?» But the water was sleeping. «Gwak, gawk,» cried seven geese, emerging from a corner. «Are you interrogating your servant? Don't you know the water is all ours; that its science belongs to us? It can only reflect our steps, our flight.» And they broke into seven pieces the water's silence. «Well, everyone talks like me, doesn't it seem?» the skeleton said. «You won't be able to separate me from you, our embrace is supreme. You'll never know me completely, nor name nor break my embrace. Let's make peace.» «You are mud and I hate you,» I responded. «Prisoner of the fear of feeling you, I sense you hidden and about to appear, you are mine and at the same time I don't know you. You never dare show your ugliness in the flesh, and I am your mask. Who will free me from your presence? Perhaps I will ask Aglaia.» «Since when do you believe in her ability?» the skeleton noted ironically. «But I won't deny myself entry to your enclosures. May she preside over this quarrel.» And we went through the miracle door.

«I always sensed you so alone, so small and alone, between the trembling of the candles in the gloom of your chapel, the vacillating clamors, the tearless moaning,» Aglaia said. «The ruptured eye cannot wet its prayer,» I said: «how welcome you this? Leave me to clear the gold of your altar with this present you have always possessed. If my gift does not buy your thaumaturgy I will talk to you of the sun, of the magnolias, of the water. You do not know all these things, despite your power, since the gloom envelops you, and at your side there is a cloister, and life, and you cannot turn around and see them. I will talk to you of that, and my eyes will serve as your guide while you allow me to regard the  skeleton, this death I wear within me, a death I tow forever. And I want to know it, in order to name it and free myself of it. The magnolias are in such bloom!» «How will I see what you say, if my eyes were plucked out in martyrdom?» Aglaia asked me. «I don't have eyes, but I lift my sockets to heaven and do not know if I'm gazing at full brightness or into the void. And those who believe in that which I love do not feel your worry.» «If you feel this way it is that you do not believe in he whom she loves,» the skeleton, between laughs, concluded. «You've failed miserably, let's go.» And we returned to the cloister. The geese pecked at the moon's radiance in the drops that sprinkled down from the fountain. I stopped for a moment to contemplate them, and then, suddenly, picked up my pace again. «Never, never in my life have you felt this heavy to me,» I said to my skeleton. «I can barely drag you, you load!» «Charity for a blind man,» psalmed a shadow at the door of the cloister. «May the saint save you all from this misfortune. Seeing or doing first is not everything.» «The palm is so jealous of us!» sang still the magnolias. «It is yellow from so much envy and you cannot do anything, anything at all but stoke it. Her passion bewitches us. But what would become of us without the envy of the palm?» they concluded, shaking their ultra-green foliage with delight. «The magnolias also speak like the skeleton. And the water, and the geese, the blind man, the palm, and Aglaia,» I sadly thought. «Almost, I almost love you. Perhaps it is you whom I love,» my skeleton offered. «Yes. Will you accept, this once, my embrace?» it rejoiced. «What do you want me to say, what choice do I have,» I said. And we accompanied each other, already close friends, through the streets and around the corners, conquering obstacles made of moon and shadow.

# Myrrha

«O, dixit, felicem, conjuge matrem!»[6]

Ovid, *Metamorphoses*, X, 422

«Ni tampoco pienses que algún caso de
amores espantara mi vejez, pues tu gentileza
y mocedad te excusan de ser culpada.»[7]

Cristóbal de Villalón, *Tragedia de Mirrha*

# I

«Do you understand? Do you understand?» Myrrha said to the
horrified old nurse. «You don't have the guts to say the damned

---

6    "O, Mother," she said, "how happy in your husband!"
7    Nor think it some case of love frigtening away my old age, for your
kindness and youth accuse you of being to blame.

word. Crime, incest: these are empty words to me; some say that in other places these words have no meaning. And I have to be condemned for the sake of some unjust law? I'm forbidden from what's most likely good for the blacks? The gods have a double precept according to skin-color for just this very situation? The beasts breed among themselves without a thought of blood relations, and they, too, are the work of the immortals. Reason and racial pedigree put roadblocks in the way of our desires? Ai, old nurse, as if! If my passion is a sacrilege, then let me follow the dark path to the Three Sisters. O free me, with your art, to love Cinyras. Because I love him.» «I have lived through much, and almost nothing scares me,» the old nurse answered. «But this is too much. Don't you know that what you desire violates the most sacred laws of the gods?» «Don't judge, old nurse, clutching at Jurisprudence with your concepts, because they're malleable. No sermons, dear. Words have no content to me, and, as you already know, I have a ton of them at my disposal. You were responsible for my knowing Cinyras, and so leave my soul tied to its destiny.» «And what's that?» asked the old nurse. «A word that just came to me,» Myrrha responded. «I'll offer it to the philosophers.» «In their hands you'll end up with a fine muddle, praise be to the gods,» said the old nurse. «As I don't want you to die,» she added, «and I am trying to see myself in your position (you are young, pretty, and Cinyras is still rather handsome), a mere shaken crumb, I will take your side. I will help you. From top to bottom, there is not a single order established by the gods that cannot be trespassed, with their blessing. May the Silent Ones be in your favor, child.» «Thank you,» Myrrha said.

# II

And came the days of the Cerealia. And Cenchreis, mother of Myrrha, as is custom, left the palace to worship these days. And therefore, Myrrha, helped by the old nurse, could finally satisfy her passion.

«Are you pleased?» the old nurse asked after the first night. «Extremely so, yes, I'm happy. Now I know the worth of what we call life. Approaching the bed I stumbled three times, but Cinyras' arms made me forget the sinister omens. How handsome and strong Cinyras is, an inexhaustible hero!» «It is all for a good purpose, child. Nevertheless, the omens are sinister. We are trespassing the law, despite no blood having yet been spilled. May Magaera and the other two circle far from your head. And far from mine,» the old nurse said.

# III

«And that scares you?» the eunuch asked the old nurse. «Here in our country it's business as usual. The bond of love is strengthened by so many complex knots, and is so strong that not even the gods can destroy it.» The smeared black skin shone in the darkness. «But you don't know how to guard a secret, old woman: you're a chatterbox. Why have you come to blabber to me about this story? I have other things more important to do than listen to you.» He hushed for a moment, deep in thought, and then laughed. «And anyway, old woman, I fear that the anecdote isn't really so over the top, not even when judged according to the laws of your own people. Don't you recall, lady, that, just before becoming expectant with Myrrha, Cenchreis loved? And not, I believe, Cinyras; not at all.» A footstep was heard in the darkness. «Shh, it's Myrrha!» the old nurse said, shocked.

# IV

«How miserable, how miserable I am!» moaned Myrrha. «Is what the black said true?» she asked. «I'm not certain,» the old nurse responded, timidly. «But then again it was talked about, and someone was brave enough to make a mockery of Cinyras.» «Useless, doddering twit!» cried Myrrha. «And I had to give up my integrity, my shame? And here I was thinking I had violated the most severe law of the Silent Ones! Now I'll be the laughing-stock of gods and men. All of this is your fault, old woman; but listen to me: if I die, you will have to go before me down the path to the Shadow.» «Certainly not!» shrieked the old nurse. «Myrrha, princess, what is it that you're after? Forget the words of the slave, rumors. I will tell you, under oath, the true word: Cenchreis never knew another man but Cinyras.» «The handsome, strong, powerful Cinyras, the inexhaustible hero!» Myrrha exulted, already more calm. And the two women disappeared down the corridor toward the chamber. «And Ovid tells what happened next,» Efrem Pedagog, salivating, lectured. And he decided to continue the story. «Hey!» said Senyora Maria Castelló, cutting him off suddenly. And no one added a single word more.

# On Orthodoxy

Upon entering the world, all of us respected the harmonic balance of these three axioms (or things that were considered as such until then): «The legitimacy of every individual's paternal origin is luckily unverifiable.» «The lion is king of the jungle.» And «There is nothing new under the sun.» But Joan Vulgar asked himself one day: «Is there nothing, absolutely nothing new, under the sun?» His characteristic, vacillating speech made its way to the ears of Ecolampadi Miravitlles. «Everything is old,» assured Ecolampadi with sufficient resignation. «Everything?» Joan Vulgar asked with reticence. «Hmm! Well, it's not altogether clear.» And he smiled. «You have a secret. I can feel it. Let it out,» ordered Ecolampadi Miravittles. «Who, me?» Joan Vulgar responded with shock. «Not that I'm aware of. Only . . . » «Ah, I get it; you're brilliant!» Ecolampadi Miravittles cried out enthusiastically. «Joan Vulgar has just discovered that not everything is old under the sun.» And he hastened to evangelize his wife and friends. «Yes?» welcomed Ventura, his dignified wife. «Me, I'm happy, so very happy.» And so he went on, submerged in his little domestic arrangement. Friends reacted in another way. «This man, your acquaintance, must possess a splendid intelligence. I would like you to present him to me,» Efrem Pedagog insisted. «Joan Vulgar,» Ecolampadi Miravitlles began his introduction, «as you no doubt already know . . . Efrem Pedagog.» «Come closer, young man. There is absolutely nothing vulgar about what it is in your head. You shall go very far; and I shall take you under my wing.» And Efrem protectively patted Joan on the back. «So you say that not everything is old under the sun? Life, totalitarian.» «I don't say all of that, sir,» Joan Vulgar modestly interjected. «I don't affirm, I ask. A question mark, if that pleases you. It's all otherwise. Only an insinuation, an insinuation, sir.» «False!» cried Ecolampadi Miravitlles. «Pay no attention to what he is saying to you, Efrem. He does not ask, he affirms. I am the most orthodox, the first to whom the new idea descended. Is this not true, Ventura?» «I don't recall,» answered the wife. «I'm always doing the laundry.» «That does not matter,» Efrem Pedagog said curtly. «Young man, I free you from disorder, and I shelter you.» «Thank you,» Joan Vulgar, with reverence, said.

And his gospel triumphantly made its way around the world, and Joan Vulgar's fame spread far enough to anger Efrem. «Well,» Pedagog began, rigorously, in thought,  «Well, does Joan Vulgar make an affirmation or is he resigned to questioning? This point is vital, we shall clarify our positions.» And he wrote up a tract of twenty-two books, with the title: *De universali ordine vel Nihil novum sub sole.* «Efrem envies Joan Vulgar,» Ecolampadi Mirravitlles observed. «It's reproachable to assure that he alone queries. What maliciousness! Joan Vulgar affirms.» «Do you think so?»

insinuated the founder. «Quiet. What do you know about this?» Ecolampadi demanded. «Did I not feel before anyone else that I am not orthodox?» «Yes, but . . . » began Joan Vulgar. «Let it go. Your doctrine doesn't keep me up at night!» the disciple said, cutting him off. And he wrote the voluminous *De orthodoxia seu De fide Joannis Vulgaris disputatio.* «Efrem Pedagog envies Joan Vulgar,» the public cried out. «Off to the Viuviuvescu to find the cause of it.» And thus the process went up to the plenary session. The Viuviuvescu, which in that era was staggering through a conflict over the regional nomenclature, studied the case with great care and found Pedagog guilty, sentencing him to silence. And thus increased the glory of Joan Vulgar.

That is, until another from the school of Efrem, the eloquent Crisant Baptista Mestres took to stirring the ashes. «Ok, we have learned what Joan Vulgar affirms,» formulated Crisant. «And, in exchange, we ignore what is new under the sun, and that, gentlemen, seems to me more of the essence.» «Silence, I say,» flared Ecolampadi Miravitlles. «What is new under the sun? What's new?» he sought. «Miravitlles, I fear I have thought up a new fuss,» said Joan Vulgar in that precise moment. «They say the lion is the king of the jungle. The king of the jungle? Who believes that?» «Do you believe that, my good fellow?» Ecolampadi asked Crisant in a preemptive tone. «I have not considered this problem, I am not a naturalist,» the eloquent Crisant confessed with uneasiness. «And you have the pretension to demand that those things new under the sun specify themselves to you, when you can't answer doubts as to whether the lion is or is not the king of the jungle!» the orthodox Miravittles said, ridiculing him. «It is not,» Mrs. Verity Experimental said, as she arrived. «It is not: *ibi non sunt leones*. I've been there,» she assured. And Joan Vulgar figured it all out by pure speculative force. «Bless me,» Ecolampadi, as he kneeled down, requested. «Your sectarian fervor is paradigmatic, acolyte,» granted the god Joan Vulgar. «But refrain from sharing it with me now; I am worried. Tula wrote me from Havana to say that she awaits me and thinks so much about me. I have not seen her in well over a year. Will she deceive me? I'll die, because I love her, I love her,» Joan Vulgar cried. «Everything is permitted you,» Ecolampadi said to calm him. «You are not a man. The laws of nature obey you, you can trespass them or transform them as you will. And when I visited Tula a couple of moths ago we talked . . . » «Don't add any more,» interjected Joan Vulgar, the god. «You have lifted a weight from me. I just find it strange, a little strange.» And he moved away. «If I am not permitted this third indisputable proposition, which is the first!» murmured Ecolampadi Miravitlles with a worried air, and during an excusably jittery moment. And on the other hand, faith, including the most substantive theocentric beliefs—and the faith of Miravitlles, rock-solid, generative, Pauline, was certainly such—is a gift that no merit can buy or conquer, always as fragile as the finest crystal, thin as a cat's ear at its most erect.

# The Heart of the Town

«I demand a bed to die in,» the bitter man cried out. «A bed, gentlemen. It's not much. On the other hand, I'm within my rights.» The fever had him in a fog and he took, suddenly, to singing enormities made up of the aftertaste of bitter extremism. «Grab that subversive!» the people protested. «A bed, what pretensions! And what does he want one for? Before dying, without a doubt, for his indiscretions. This is intolerable. Detain him!» At that moment, the defeated man fell silent, and suddenly, without warning, vomited a profuse red substance. «Wine dregs,» opined Ròmul Serafí Catarneu. «Blood, no: he'd be complaining again. The guy in the bed is running a scam. I see what he's up to. There's still not a person around who can fool me, daughter. So much making a scene and spinning around in circles, no one can make me look bad.» «You rascal!» Anneta Quintana said, censuring him. «Inveterate! Can't you see the poor man is dying of hunger?» And she disappeared. She returned in no time at all, eagerly, with a glass of milk. «Drink it, you have to make good use of it,» she offered it, maternally, to him. «Good expenditure,» verified Senyora Magdalena Blasi, who was passing by. «My goodness! A glass of milk, not even watered down, equivalent to a certain financial sacrifice.» «And I'm nothing more than a poor embroiderer,» stressed the sweet altruist. «Nevertheless, I add my soul.» «You hath chosen wisely: Jew for Jew, God. He will pay thee for it, and for many years,» wished Senyora Magdalena Blasi, as she moved on. «My Jesus, in Thee I confide,» Anneta Quintana, crying out, said. «Now that he has revived and the vomit's dried up, perhaps the just thing to do is detain him,» some passersby decided. And in one dense group they carried him to the Commissar. «His offense? Your name?» asked that honorable man. «My information is unimportant,» breathed the vagabond. «Procedure,» the honorable man, enunciating precisely, said. «He demanded a bed to die in. He said insolent things,» the witnesses revealed. «A bed? You're being ridiculous,» the Commissar said, puzzled. «Ha, ha, ha, our chief gets it, this man is ridiculous,» the subordinates laughed, all of them, down to the last one. «More absurd than criminal,» the Commissar said, free, by his judgment, to ironize. «Yes, more absurd than criminal,» the subordinates unanimously agreed. «Then won't you grant me a bed?» the pale beggar asked. The honorable man turned furious. «Indeed not!» he yelled. «It's just as well you've been detained for causing a commotion in public.» «Put me away,» urged the idler. «In order to maintain you, serve you, free of cost, I imagine? Out!» the honorable man bellowed. The hall had been emptying. Salom approached the unhappy man. «Where will you go now?» he half-sympathized with him. «Are you with the press?» the misfortunate man asked. «They say that the press is organizing a campaign for cases like mine.» «I'm a publicist. No one, however, reads my work,» Salom sighed. «Charity-should-become-a-state-service,» he quickly added to attenuate his hardly flattering declaration. «I admire the originality of the concept,» the beggar said, «but I'm not thinking of swindling it from you; you can rest at ease.» «Well, what would you like me to tell you,» Salom said. «Charity has to be statized, to be statized.» And he repeated, with that innocence of his, this verb, hardly academic these days. «I believe in the heart of the town. Personal initiative doesn't naturally arrive everywhere. The State . . . » «And in the meantime?» the one man, interrupting the other, asked. «You're talking about a hypothesis, like in a book. And in the meantime, I ask you?» «And in the meantime, perhaps you're right,» Salom meditatively said. «In the meantime you're not left with anything more than the drama of the street. And what if you scattered your lungs into pieces across the most sumptuous parts of Lavínia? When all is said and done, you waste them with coughing fits. Take care of them.» «Stupid solutions of a romantic writer: squash flies with a sledgehammer, charge giants with a frying pan. The opulence of Lavínia, from the pulse of an unalterable rhythm, from an unstaggering solidity of the gut and liver, manipulates diverse measuring sticks that with tactical precision accommodate and change its inviolable interests. And it's changed them all behind my back with so much dialectical rigor that they've pierced me to the marrow of the bone of my conviction. What has never been measured nor needs be measured, not even with the most sordid meanness, is the value, always null and void by my reckoning, of my lungs. And less so when I already no longer have it,» the sick man responded. And he choked, spit out his last morsel, and gave his life in testimony to his truth. «Exemplary punishment for a culprit of anthrophobia,» Salom, scandalized and offended, said. «To the memory of my deceased. Five pesetas for the bed of the penniless patient. Coloma Marés, widow of Cal·licó,» filtered out of an archaic radio in a corner. «The heart of the town has to be trusted,» Salom said optimistically. And he looked at the wasted away body and left. He couldn't be delayed, and he didn't deserve to freeze to death either.

# Hildebrand

That disastrous-looking man said:

«You want to know my past? Here's to not breaking up this illustrious gathering: I am a new murderer of shadow, and my shadow was named Hildebrand. I met him in the French Legion, where I ended up due to romantic circumstances. One wretched afternoon, in Le Houga, in the middle of the desert, he set out to find me. We were fifty lost souls, depression was driving us mad; we hardly had water. I'd never paid attention to him before. At least not in any particular way, and he emerged suddenly, as if he were arriving in the capacity of my protector. He offered me his ration of liquid, and the blues and gratitude made me accept it. Great evil that he was, he knew the power of an opportunely compassionate attitude. He dominated me, he enslaved me, he turned me into an automaton. He mocked me; he took pleasure in irritating me so that I'd feel my impotence. I hated him and I couldn't free myself from him. He dragged me beyond the bounds of the law, and under his orders I had to commit low crimes, repugnant offenses. At times I ask myself why he chose me as his victim. Did he suppose I was weak? I don't know, but he tortured me with refinement. He made me learn in a year and a half—by heart and in Chinese—without my understanding a word of it, Li-Ping's *The Abridged Commentaries of Lao-Tse*, a work of a mere forty-seven volumes, and he obliged me to recite it whenever he had insomnia. On another occasion, at a cannibal festival, he demanded I devour the gall bladder and rib of a leprous old sorcerer from a tribe of the Balolo, dead from the bite of a bluebottle fly. I can't look at turtles, they make me nauseous: Hildebrand amused himself, for two months, with the contemplation of the trembling provoked in me each day—once I'd been tied up so that I couldn't move—by the slow stroll of the most abominable exemplar of that species across my exposed belly. Why tell of my horrors? He hypnotized me, he enslaved me, and he was slight in build, while I, as you can see, am quite corpulent. We wandered the streets, for years and years, an eternity. He was the devil, my shadow, a blue nightmare. Until I murdered him in Lavínia, at the doors of Santa Maria Liberal.»

He paused to breathe and to smoke. The man continued:

«Hildebrand, or the spirit of contradiction: connoisseur of anti-things. If I affirmed any historical date, because I'm college-educated, he would correct me, hunkered down in voguish German research, and he would underline an error to me for ten hours. If I exalted Caesar or Alexander, he would bring up the existence of a tremendous (and of course unmatched) Incan, Sioux, or Macanese-Portuguese captain. He restrained my enthusiasm for a grand literary figure with the bitterness of his precise erudition: the grand figure plagiarized an obscure author who was the legitimate star. He corrected me, he shamed me, he knew the last secret and the latest discovery of the latest school of thought. He understood wines, watches, philosophy, cacti, jurisprudence, medicine and the music of Bach, Buddhist *eudaimonia*, and fifty thousand other things. He was a competent orator, the future of Humanity, past tense of the animal branch itself, passing for stylistic French distinction and *joie de vivre*, and the feminine heart. With his experience he would have been a really sharp film critic. My God, how he counter-asserted! In Syracuse, in the catacombs of S. Giovanni, he and a friar who was accompanying us argued about the name of the bones of the martyrs that were buried there. Naturally, the conversation degenerated into an examination of the dates conserved regarding the coming of Saint Paul to Rome and the analysis of the scientific solvency of the evidence traditionally presented to this end. An hour from Lassa, he argued with Jetsunma Neel about the properties of a few syntactical varieties of "Kyapdo." Jetsunma, from drowsiness, was about to cross the benedictions of Nub-dewa-Tsxen. In Debra Libanos he lost himself with the Abun Iasú in an endless digression on the wonders of Saint Tekla Haimanot. The Abun wanted to have him burned, and it's a shame that he escaped it. In Kairouan, in the Mosque of the Sabers, he couldn't manage to agree with Ishaq ibn Mansur, snake charmer, from the Mālikī school. They spoke of the meanings of "adl" within the general "Sahadic" system. Ishaq defended Ibn Arafah's definition as correct. Hildebrand opposed him with Ad-Dardir. Ishaq accused him of "hawarig." They reconciled at the end of the neutral, limitative camp of the four Kaba'ir.»

«Eh!» Trinquis said, growing impatient, getting fed up.

That pitiful-looking man said:

«Pardon, I will keep it brief. One day we arrived in that great country Konilòsia. In Lavínia, our city, the most beautiful dance is danced, literature of the highest standard produced, and the town is probably conscientious by obligation, and totalitarian against its will. There, I met a girl.»

He paused to cough. Then continued:

«A girl with large eyes, slender then. She loved me, we married, we were happy. But Hildebrand, who desired her, worked diligently through the night. He organized a systematic campaign to discredit me. The woman was very religious. One day, Hildebrand steered the conversation toward the Inquisition. We argued. About this I had clear ideas, principles: the Inquisition, you all know it, etc. He made himself into an apologist for it. Full of shock, the woman found me hardly fervent, and she devoted herself to Hildebrand.»

Then he said:

«This shame liberated me. Here's how it happened: Hildebrand had, a few days later, an exceptionally laborious bout of indigestion. He obliged me to leave with him, to help him. He had been drinking. We walked a while in silence. Suddenly, he took to conceitedly glorifying his conquest. He exasperated me, but the custom of servitude impeded me from acting out. And then rang the hour of my liberation. Hildebrand, and this was unusual, began to tell me things in confidence. I had never heard a thing about him, about his life. That afternoon I learned everything. And as he showed me his soul, his influence disappeared, and I recovered my will. From external, historical confidences we moved to the most intimate of details. "You know?" Hildebrand said to me. "I have sixty-three red spots on my skin, from the nape of my neck to my waist." The self-importance in this I found unbearable. "No!" I responded. "Surely you don't have that many, let's count them." He had transferred to me his spirit of contradiction. Turning pale, he tried to recover his position. He coaxed back his old voice and insulted me: "Ask your lady. She . . . " He didn't finish. At the doors of Santa Maria Liberal, my knife found the depths of his heart.»

«You talk too much,» Trinquis, who was presiding, interrupted. «You're a college guy, pedantic, absurd, and a liar. Now you'll shut up and listen to stories from leprous lips.»

We okayed the beggars and stoked bonfires by the sea-fog. A train passed staggering along the neighboring track, and we made out, behind the windows, the blanched faces of passengers, faces like ghosts. And perhaps they were dead.

# Thanatos

*In memory of my uncle, Mutsu-Hito, who told me this story.*

It was time. And it was stretched through the space of days and months, with unnecessary cruelty, and the suffering was prolonged, and the meager savings dried up. It was no doubt the hour. The hopeful lightning was definitively exiled; all of the remedies were going bankrupt. All that remained was the cruel reality of the carcass, a few bones struggling against death. Where did the spirit rest? Far, far, a little light amid the gloom, panting light, eaten orbits, face of wax. And, what's more, she has her head clear, the sticking-in-the-throat of the last hour, a recommendation on the tips of the lips, useless. Until she recognizes the others: her sister, those who ask, the indifferent ones. Indifferent ones? All of them, all of them strange, outside, external, alive. Her, her alone in the fight, without assistance, and her spirit was always so weak! Would no one save her now? They can't leave her, they can't leave her, onward, win, it's already time!

Bitter life. Poor, sad, difficult life. She and her sister, alone. The others in the family, scattered. The others? Them, them alone, all two of them, poor old women. Bitter life, slow life that approaches, humble, indefectible, wasteland, on time. Do you promise that when it comes, when it comes, solemn bells will ring, face to face? And there will be many priests, rich responses, candles. And the coffin, at least double, the inside made of zinc, do you promise? No wood: the reinforcements zinc. I think that's why I worked, that's why I suffered, that's why I lived. Will you make it so, do you promise? And the tunic, silk, that one in the drawer, bridal silk or shroud silk. Shroud! Shroud, a few whacks, shoveling, silence. The sun, out. The singing, out. Pain, out. All of me, alone. All of me, rotting. All of me, awaiting the chill of time. And you're crying? Sister, sister, you're no longer useful to me, sister! The spirit, far, far from here, to the other side, where you won't be able to follow me. Not at all right now, now no, after, I don't know when, also alone, when another time arrives. This is mine, all for me, the only thing I fully live for, alone. To live at the very moment of death! What do you know about whether it's a justification for me, if it cleanses me of my sins? Humble, vegetative sins, sins of misfortune, without bravery. Flabby envy, tiny desires, risking little. Risk? If nothing has been had that was hers, that was hers! Not a stare, nor a hug from a male, nor a little bit of luxury. She and her sister. She and her sister, inseparable: same words, same clothes, same urges, identical tears. Years and suffering, years and suffering, a vulgar and gray, enduring monotony. Passing has to be dealt with, cent after cent—money fades away and it's necessary to save for old age, for epidemic illness, for when the time comes, this, that has already arrived. It's useless, all useless, sister: the tears, the prayers, the Christ. Kisses, kisses? Yes, don't make me queasy, three or four, don't make me queasy. Alone, the Christ, kisses, three or four.

She died, they dressed her, out of custom they sought the mantilla, but her sister wants it, wants this one, because it's a good one, a doily, and she wants it for herself, to go to mass, for when the other time, hers, comes. Poor girl! What would you do with it, poor girl? Sepulchre, modest burial, but not without a sense of luxury, poor girl, because she toiled and deserved it. Cancer, suffering, months and months, poor girl. All for naught.

—And of the two sisters, the one who remains is the more shameful. The other, whatever, it's already over for her, God may have pardoned her. What are you saying? He wiped it all clean! The other, kick her out. Yes, the living one. Black!

Once more associated with her sister, the living one, who solicits and monopolizes shame. And is this my time? If it's also time for her—not her time, but yes, time for her. You plan for that, dream about that? Disaster.

Raised cross, Latin magic of those days, extremely short retinue of remote cousins and the occasional neighbor. While burnt-out laborers lower and carelessly close the coffin in its niche, bitter dispute of two relatives over the custody—in the care of one or the other—of the funerary title. In accordance with the norms of that vanished age, it was to go to the younger of the two for having closer ties to the deceased. Wasn't it fair?

# The Figurines of the Nativity Scene

Why were the Nativity scene figurines in the box so still? Why didn't they stir like before, eager to escape the wooden prison? They spent the entire year forgotten, silent, full of boredom and cold. How pitiful they were, the poor things, when the children spied them during their short visits, the toy soldier's and train set's brief parentheses of boredom. But the day came, and they quickly leapt up, keen to make contact with mountains of cork and to tread the sand and to take in the intimate smell of moss. They arranged them by categories, and the hierarchies were re-established, and the anarchic mix in the box was rectified. Old shepherds, harvesters, the fisherman, the spinner, the group from the cave: all bright, Hebraically garbed, with capricious turbans. They were refined, erudite, and scoffed at the simplicity of the farmers *a la catalana*. All of them with their own personalities. The boys distinguished themselves quite well and never forgot their names. Each day, until Candlemass, they were moved and transferred across long distances. That allowed them to converse with each other, and they shared pieces of gossip down to the last detail. At night they revered the newborn and entertained the parents, whose task obliged them to stay in the cave. During the adoration they informed the patriarch (the little Virgin wasn't in a good mood) of all of the quotidian anecdotes: that today the wise men had only advanced a few steps, that a camel had broken a hoof, that a fisherman boasted of the vainglory of continuous bounty, with the same fish always on the end of his rod. The patriarchal carpenter smiled, listening to them, and the entrancing wand made him prosper. The songs and naïve, infantile prayers came later. The guiding light took a mad course to the stable, perhaps already tired of its role, impatient for the definitive occasion, and the kings suddenly galloped on to capture it. The children shuffled all the wise architecture placed there by maternal hands, and carried on their bustling until it was time to go to bed. Later, already in the dark, a deathly silence extended over the Nativity scene. The injured complained and patiently awaited the following day, the panacea of an adhesive. In the middle of the night a mouse descended from its lair and walked through the avenues and streets under the rows of butcher's-broom trees, and knocked down the shepherds on its way toward the cave. It was said that the mouse was a great eater of flour-like snow, and so the following day it had to snow again over the Nativity.

Every year the children chose their favorites, the propitiatory victims, a few innocent martyrs. Those heroes experienced thrilling, cruel adventures of primitive ferocity. They were tossed from peaks of cork to test the hardness of their bodies, or submerged in the calm water of a pond until the mud began to damage them, or burned in sheaves, after unjust and extremely short trials. Once in a blue moon they'd return to the silence and oblivion of the box, but they'd won, on the other hand, a highly honorable burial, with funeral song and military parades. With the years the mausoleum grew, and the mother's economic alarm broke from the destruction, from the inevitable revival.

Few carried on whole. Some more, some less—all, even the holy personages, cried from the break of an arm, head, or leg, the loss of an eye, a roasting, or a prolonged bath. The Magi and ox-plowmen were the most affected. The children remembered, as the years passed, entire dynasties, and the excellences of the vanished were praised. And it was so each year. Each year, the weak architecture of the Nativity scene, the thrill of the countryside in full December in the city. Interior December, with the nakedness of the plane trees outside. Municipal plane trees, captive, extraordinarily sad. Evocation of a small, false spring, with moss, butcher's-broom and heath, agave and flour-like snow.

Why were they so motionless inside Salom's box of nightmares, the figurines of the Nativity scene, not stirring like before, eager to flee from the wooden prison? A shepherdess told the diaphanous secret to the aging, tired, and totally skeptical Salom, wept as she unfolded the story's disappointment, and her weeping moistened the adhesive, that remedy of great wounds, and her head fell and rolled to his feet. One of Balthazar's black pageboys took up the thread of the tale, and Salom saw himself there as in a mirror. Without children or murmur or breakage, they didn't want to go out. But since they had to come out, who would help them come out? And in that trivial nightmare of a solitary man, Salom noted a smile.

Perhaps he didn't go often to the tomb, but he remembered how the lamenting figurines—with a pretentious anachronism of pseudo-Hebraic adornment—had gone about banishing little by little from the beloved Nativities, when he was small, the modest anachronism of the figurines of farmers tidied up *a la catalana.*

# The Beheaded

*To Joaquim Molas, this version, which I want to think is
the definitive one.*

He caught my attention. I thought they'd transfer him from one
side to the other. Because, despite his prized mutilation, the man
had an exaggeratedly healthy look, apoplectic. He weighed a lot,
surely. What he was lacking in arms and legs he more than made
up for in belly and cheeks: the riffraff was the owner of just half
an arm and half a foot, limbs, as can be seen, scarce and otherwise
poorly distributed. The atrophied, experienced foot stuck out of
him, dangling just beside his right haunch. The arm . . . Allow
me to tell you about it: rickety, consumptive, sown with eruptive
spots. And, with everything, the honest fellow evinced a decided
air of happiness. He faced the sun, propped in his habitual corner.
It seemed he was asking for crumbs of cash out of an uncontrol-
lable collector's passion. A type of wooden plate held the fat figure
up and isolated him from the municipal slabs. I accustomed my-

self to considering the cripple as a decorative element of the street, a monstrous plant. But how could they carry him from one place to another? The mystery obsessed me, and I lay in wait. And lo and behold, one day, finally, I saw. A lean young man neared the misfortunate fellow and passed a showy jumble of cords across his body. He loaded the bundle on his back and left. I followed them. It was dusk, a late foggy afternoon. «You're getting heavy,» the lean man said. «If I don't exercise I get fat,» answered, amused, the piece of a man. His locomotive system toiled in silence for a while. «Uf!, I don't know what's going on with you today, I'm soaked,» the lean man said, shortly. «You're at least carrying some serious cash, right, buddy?» The halved man excused himself, humbly: «The good souls don't pay any attention to me anymore, the business has thinned out.» «Dammit! We ought to choose a new spot!» this interesting locomotive subject thought. «If you fail me, I'll leave you a quarter of a slice of bread for the entire day, so you get it into your head. It's good for the blood,» he added. «This heat is stifling, I'm going to cool down; I'll be right back,» the lean man finished, relieving himself of the cripple. And he took off. He left him hanging over the handrail of a balcony at the mouth of an abyss. «And if he moves!» I thought. And I drew nearer. «That isn't a place to stop,» I yelled out to him. «Courage, I'll get you out of there.» «No, no need, sir, don't worry, please, sir,» the poor man answered. «I'm not moving at all, poor me, I'm not going to fall. I'm getting used to it, sir. Rafaelet always leaves me on this landing. He has, and knows that he can have, confidence in me, and I haven't let him down yet,» he said with miserable pride. «Who is the person who moved you?» I asked. «Who? My brother-in-law?

88

Rafaelet: I just told you, sir. Strongman, commendable kid!» «But he treats you terribly, he abandons you,» I said. «He's thirsty, and there's a tavern near here,» the understanding cripple objected. Being a philosopher I then formulated a few fundamental questions. «What do you think of your luck—are you happy with it?» «Well, I eat,» he responded. «My goodness you're a stoic,» I told him reverently. «I don't know what that is. Are you insulting me, sir?» the man said. «Well, when all is said and done, it doesn't matter to me. But, for the love of God, if you wanted to help me out with a little bit of change, sir? Because we see tough times ahead now, and who knows if a little more food for the horse will be convenient later.» And, smiling he gestured with his short beard to the place we'd seen his brother-in-law take off for. You know well enough that I've always had an inclination toward the strangest strains of mysticism. «You, for handling misfortune the way you do, you've won everlasting peace,» I psalmed. «Well, sir, that's all fine and good. A little spare change, come on, a little pittance, I beg you,» cried out the halved man. «My saint, chosen one, lead me to God, for I am a sinner,» I let out as I fervently kissed his malignant pustules. «I see, mocking the misfortunate, that's not Christian. Not even five pesetas, just a little spare change, just a little spare change is all I ask you.» Why break my emotion with your inopportune begging? You didn't want to comprehend the sacrifice of my distinction, my subtle recognition of your superiority, and as dear as it was, it suddenly cost you. «It's still not enough that I'm kissing your wounds?» I said. «Fine, here.» And with a push I launched him down the precipice. His head rebounded against a rock and scattered in four pieces around his corpse. «What have I done?» I asked. «Am I maybe a murderer?» «Mig, don't get full of yourself,» my faithful conscience said to me with near mathematical precision. «Ah, you're right, thanks,» I said to my conscience. «You're welcome,» my conscience tidily answered. «And besides, considering you've ruined the family business.» «Oh, yes, that was really immoral!» I said, broken, when he was already in the distance. «I suspect I performed an act of mercy.» And I continued on my way. A remote uproar reached me, the moaning of Rafaelet. «Oh, luckless one, you've fallen; were you that heavy? What wind could have knocked you over? My fortune is dead, and my hope. The bread of my children, lost. Who's robbed me of my riches? Did you fall, or did an envious hand push you? Look at him there, beheaded, and that was the only part he had all of; the only part that was essential. Ai, poor, poor me!» «God is just,» I concluded, as I disappeared into the mist.

# Vulgar History

Now and again a shy voice passes by asking for the sick
man and . . . afterward departs, saying: God will provide!
Misfortune has settled there, like a shadow . . . If the
neighbor dies, misfortune shrinks down into the hard and
concrete form of a cadaver . . . And on another day he will
be buried: and the shadow will already be gone.

Miró, «Señor Vicario y Manihuel» (*Años y lenguas*)

## I

«Poor boy!»

«Poor parents!»

A group of old relatives (chiaroscuroed by their witches' beards) held vigil over the dreams of the sick boy.

«Poor parents!»

«Poor boy!»

In the long run, the monotony of fingering the rosary tired them out, distracted them. They tumbled down a slope of nosy prattling now. Night in the chamber. Above the dresser-drawer, an eager desire for a miracle lit the subtle hope of a lamp. The flame lifted the prayer of intercession until it formed an image. The fire's rising soul illuminated slightly the saint's garments and forgot, in the darkness, the bed, the panting, the distress. The mother, official sufferer, clasped her hands in a silent lament for her dying son, who was already a man, and who not long ago was fine and happy, and now he was dying, he was dying with no cure. Some blow, too many blows, as a child!

«Poor boy!»

It is a pause in the run of fragments, homage to the most important belief. They are related witches, fair in their words; they have too much experience with all of these moments. The lamp trembles (oh, no, only a little bit of air through the crack, only a little bit of air). The sick boy's forehead burns an officious hand.

«Such a hard worker.»

«There wasn't another like him!»

The doctor arrived, despairing. The rector. He said grace. Who else? Ah, enough, enough, you know! Lady Rodesinda, the mistress in charge. Pale, thin, she draws close. Is this Lliset? Poor woman, she collapsed! The old women, admiring, compassionate, supported her with reverence.

«She loved him so much!»

Preterite, of course, imperfect.

«She was his godmother.»

«And she saw him born.»

«What a great heart!»

Recovered, Rodesinda embraced the mother; crying, she made a helping gesture. Coins, not many, jingled. Everyone praised the generous impulse of the mistress.

«The kind woman!»

«She can't stand to see suffering.»

«May God pay her as well as she does the wretched.»

Some heterodox voice whispered:

«She'll bill them at the close the year.»

They objected:

«Sure. Whatever comes after, hidden, does not erase the visible present of this moment, now. The woman is a saint!»

The excessive praise ran in voluptuous droplets down that excessively thin and virginal back. She collapsed again. They carried her out.

# II

Another day:

«How do you think the boy is doing?»

«Terribly. We're not coming out of it.»

«Yes, that's it,» a philosopher said. «You're born alone, live alone, and you die alone.»

«And you must save or condemn yourself alone,» the senior rector reminded them.

«Too much work, dammit.»

Above, the witches stayed up with the dying boy.

«Poor boy!»

«Poor parents!»

And finally there came to pass what everyone, for so long, had awaited. The boy died, and they had to bury him. Spring afternoon—a pretty one. The funeral procession descended mountain paths that were beginning to be disguised by flowers. The coffin was carried by hand, and those carrying it cursed its excessive weight. The entire town followed. They stopped at the small plaza, in front of the church. The rector sang in poor Latin. Everyone became emotional from not having understood him, and prophesied that it would have one effect or another. All of a sudden, a boy escaped the watchful eye of his mother and set to playing marbles at the side of the coffin where it rested in a stretcher, under a canopy of incense, for the liturgy. The boy's startled mother judged these actions to be a bad omen, and taught the boy a lesson as he shrieked and broke the gathered sorrow. The other mother, losing her wits, yelled out:

«Yours is going to die too, you know!»

Her neighbor cursed her and distanced herself. Die? Hers? Not hers, she wouldn't allow it. And she kissed him furiously, already defending her actions. The retinue continued, arriving at the cemetery. Tears, an Our Father, heading back. The men stopped at the tavern, and the father treated. Everyone drank to the health of the deceased.

# Mama Real Lylo Vesme

It was a long, narrow, and rather dark living room. We sat down. We were stacked up in an uncomfortable heap. We adopted the poses of people watching science films. Some couldn't deflect the anguish. Others had already been there and they warned us about what we would have to see. «Silence,» our Professor demanded, and went on instructing us through an extremely long lecture. At the end he dictated to us the conduct to follow before what we were to see. «And now we can begin to introduce the infirm.» The Director of the establishment gave the adequate order. «They picked them,» Pere Màrtir Passerell, who was one of the veterans, warned. «They show the most presentable ones. But I have a good time with it, I come every year.» «Greet these gentlemen,» the Director meanwhile suggested of someone who had just entered. «Good day, he, he!» said the subject, a sort of eunuchoid. «Pau is always happy,» the Director assured. «Isn't that right, good boy?» «He, he!» Pau confirmed. «Listen closely to the question,» the Professor shouted at us. «What is it that you like the most, Pau?» «He, he!»

the eunuchoid enunciated while licking his lips. «I like them . . . »
Thus, tranquilly he expressed the enormity of things. «Ha, ha,
ha!» we laughed, unanimously. «What's so funny, eh?» Pere Màrtir
Passerell asked. «I'm telling you, I come here every year.» «Shh!»
interrupted the Professor. «These deviations in sexual instinct
constitute, write this down, one of the possible characteristics of
these pathological cases.» «He, he!» shouting himself hoarse, the
eunuchoid said. «Take him away,» the Director said decisively. Pau
disappeared and was replaced by a thin man. «I present to you
all General Bum-Bum,» the Director said. «They finally put him
away?» we, the naïve, asked. «They're confusing me,» the personality protested. «Today, I am the inventor Carboni.» «This infirm
man,» our Professor documented for us, «suffers from personality
disorders. He is, depending on the day, General Bum-Bum, Carboni, or a modest writer.» «He's not a disturbed person who en-
tertains,» stressed, sotto voce, the companioning Passerell. «I've
seen him as all three and he is not at all pleasant. If he feels like
an inventor today, he's going to bewilder you with trigonomet-
ric formulas.» «Sine A, Cosine B,» revved Carboni the inventor.
«Enough,» advised the professor. «And now you will all witness an
extremely curious case,» he continued. «A woman who seems in
her appearance as normal as any of us. She argues well. In reality
we don't know whether she is or is not sick. We have her under
observation.» «They already had her there last year,» Pere Màrtir
Passerell informed us. «The rigor and logic of her mind are excellent.» A highly distinguished woman entered. She greeted us
courteously and explained that she had been there for a year; her
husband had had her locked away. That she and her husband had

never understood each other, and that she suspected that on more than one occasion she had gotten in his way. That she was fine. That, if she remained locked up, she would perhaps end up not fine. That she hoped we might feel sorry for her. That she enjoyed our visit, despite finding the group a little large. That she hoped we might not forget her. And that we might free her from her prison. «She's not demented,» we, the novices, said, moved. «Well,» countered the more clever among us headed by Pere Màrtir Passerell. «It's very suspicious that she speaks so coherently.» «Agreed,» we agreed. And we went over other illustrations of amnesia, abulia, echopraxia, echomotism. «Ha, ha!» laughed Pere Màrtir Passarell. «Boys, you're about to hear some screaming,» he promised us. They had introduced an old man. «How many years old would you all calculate this old man to be?» the Professor asked us. «Octogenarian? He hasn't even turned fifty.» «Fifty!» we were amazed. Our surprise satisfied the Director, the Professor, and the veterans. «This man suffered a formidable attack of apoplexy. He was a strong, good-looking man, and was transformed into this. He passes hour after hour immobile. Suddenly, he begins to utter some words, always the same, rather low, in a confusing tone, and goes on raising his voice, little by little. He repeats what he's saying until he reaches the point of exhaustion, and it's not at all easy to get him to be quiet. If you all had heard him, he would have impressed you. Eh, Francesc?» «Mama real lylo vesme,» he exhaled, in an extremely low voice, that wreck. «Mama real lylo vesme, Mama real lylo vesme, Mama real lylo vesme, Mama real lylo vesme.» A monotonous, obsessive song. «Lylo vesme?» we weren't familiar with it. «Ha, ha!» laughed Pere Màrtir Passerell. «Right now it's difficult to understand, but he's only saying that his mother, who died years ago, really loves him.» «Mama real lylo vesme, Mama real lylo vesme, Mama real lylo vesme,» Francesc bellowed, like a storm. «Ha, ha, ha!» pondered Pere Màrtir Passerell. «Each academic year I come here, and next year, as usual, there's no way I'm letting myself miss this,» concluded, while choking with laughter, the humorist Pere Màrtir Passerell, with whom—as with many other of my counterparts, both women and men—I had long ago pierced, without realizing it, the threshold of an arid road between high and unique barriers of imbecility and crime. And in my conscience, the thought—unbent in the western wind facing the wall —was itself already completely alone in the emptiness; stupid perversity, stupid malevolence.

# Prologue to the Devil's Ballet

«A woman in love provided me with the opportunity of meeting the demon.» «What arts did you make use of, warlock?» asked Melània, who wanted me to initiate her. «Needle, mud and a little bit of blood, sinister weapons. I won't tell you, my love, the crime that has allowed me to cross your door,» I said to her. «Gutruda came to find me.

"He hosts a dance and presents a ballet, a ballet of hypotheses. The *Six dames en noir* will be there," Gutruda warned.

»We walked along a path surrounded by abysses.

"Throw stones. For the dead," Gutruda recommended. And I threw hundreds, thousands, of stones; such was the multitudinous number of dead there! The spirits buzzed at our return.

"That's enough," Gutruda ordered. "Unless you're proposing to organize a fateful revolution with them."

"I'm not strong enough," I responded, flattered. "First I want to meet him."

»We reached a trifurcated crossroad. Gutruda traced a circle.

"Who summons me?" a voice said.

"Worship," Gutruda ordered. We bowed down.

"Don't reveal yourself, Prince, in some bloodcurdling medieval form," I prayed. "My modern sensibility wouldn't be able to handle it."

"Ok," the voice conceded.

"Nor," I dared another demand, "come adorned in a tuxedo with a high hat and an Egyptian cigarette between your lips. I've never been able to take you seriously like that, it makes me laugh."

"Dammit!" said the voice, slightly anxious. "How, then? I'm going to the ball and I have to get dressed up. You have to know I can't—I'm not allowed to—choose too many outfits."

"He seems broken up about it, don't get him overexcited," Gutruda admonished. "If he's inclined to have it rain my clothes are going to be ruined."

"He wouldn't dare," I said.

"Oh, he's quite the beast," Gutruda said.

»Lightning on the horizon.

"Fine," I conceded, in order to calm the conjurer. "You can show up in a dress coat if you'd like, Mr. Devil. How does that sound?"

»A skillful piece of shoddy stage machinery helped a middle-aged man rise from the ground.

"Thank you," he said to me meticulously. We shook hands.» «I've seen this demon act more than once, some years ago,» Melània cut in. «He was played by one of the Barrymore brothers.» «You're right,» I granted. «Those brothers had some type of exclusive run.» «Carry on, » ordered Melània. «And we shook hands.»

«"And now," the devil said, highly refined, "hurry, all of you. We'll be late to the ball, and the *Six dames en noir* are very punctual."

"And the seventh?" I asked.

"Never seen her. Never stirs from a mysterious seat of honor in the kingdom of night," the veteran Gutruda said.

"The seventh is a boy who's lost his eye," sang the devil, full of literary remembrances. Meanwhile, the path had become populated by demonic fauna: toads, lizards, slugs, bugs, snakes.

"Day after day these animals grow more numerous," observed the devil while walking with caution. "They'll get to the point where they won't be any fun for me at all, especially the snakes. I get so tempted by them!"» «Such a scatterbrained wisecrack is unworthy even of you,» Pulcre Trompel·li said dismissively. «Talking about the devil is dangerous, although not nearly as dangerous as talking about God,» sermonized Father Silví Saperes. «Snakes scare me, too,» said Melània, tying together the broken thread. «Go back to the road you traveled and introduce me, at the party, to the *Six dames en noir*. How were they dressed?» «Later. What I'm telling you is only the prologue,» I warned. «Well that's enough for today, eh?» Melània pleaded. «You're the boss,» I said, relieved. «Don't play with fire. Not even with imitations,» benevolent Senyora Maria Castelló counseled from the high, distant peak of her death.

# My Friend Salom

«Yes,» said my friend Salom of Konilòsia (an observation for the good Frenchman: that exotic land that lies between Rarotonga and the Sea of Dreams). «Yes, I'm happy now, but it cost me.» He explained to us the process behind his battles. «I was born,» he explained, «forty-five years ago in a great city in Konilòsia. You all, being from a normal country, will with difficulty understand what happens in that remote region. The Konilòsians, people of a glorious history, otherwise like the glorious histories of all people, tumbled and still tumble down an endless slope. They're distrustful, cheap, and pitiful. They treat spiritual as well as material shared heritage with the greatest possible indifference. Now they believe themselves an inferior people in every way, now they adopt an attitude of ridiculous arrogance. The Konilòsians never read anything ever, know nothing, are interested in nothing, but God save you from bumping into an erudite Konilòsian—and there are some—because you would see how he mixes Goethe with an anthology of nonsense. They are envious and stingy, they praise the powerful and the mediocre, they tolerate neither talent nor independence of character, and any snobbish foreigner discovers from time to time some forgotten and secular Konilòsian value.»

Having arrived at this point, Salom took a small pause, then suddenly continued:

«As I told you, I was born in Lavínia—a great city, yes, a great city—and within the nationalist focus of the Lavínians, those who formed a separate group within Konilòsia. They have a different language and all of the defects of the Konilòsians, augmented. The Lavínians work in commerce, under a coarse and fundamental exploitation of manufacturing and the law, which fattens and stuffs our abundant, smart, and clever fauna. The Lavínians are the rich of Konilòsia.» «Don't digress so much,» I warned him. «It's true, pardon me,» Salom conceded. «I'll look to limit myself to the thread of the narrative, which carries me again to Lavínia, where I spent my infancy and my youth. I was studious, always surrounded by books. People began to look at me askance, praising me in public but thinking something entirely different to themselves, as is the tendency in Lavínia.

"So, what will the good kid become when he grows up?"

"A lawyer, like his father."

»And I graduated with a law degree.

"Now on to practice," my father said.

»But the lectures had turned my brain upside down.

"No, papa." I responded. "I don't like law; I'm thinking to reach higher."

"You mean you might go into commerce?" my progenitor asked, somewhat hopefully.

"No, I want to reform Lavínia, Konilòsia, and all these things."

"You'll ruin yourself, lazy," my father said.

»I smiled smugly. And I ruined myself.«

Salom was silent for a moment and then continued:

«Yes, I ruined myself. Me, the redeemer. For ten, fifteen, twenty years, I swam against the current. Do you know what that's like? Do you know how the fight gets drained out of you by the wickedness, the hypocrisy, and the ignorance of Lavínia?

"You and you and you all, etc., you're all so and so and so other, etc.," I accused them severely.

"Who do you think you are, why are you saying this to us?" they responded at the beginning. "Antipatriot!"

"I like the indignation. When all is said and done you'll correct yourselves," I said, very happy. "But that doesn't erase your defects."

"Your mother!" they later said. And they started to whistle at me and mock me.

"Ai, modify yourselves, you'll condemn each other before history, you'll die as a nation if you insist on continuing this way," I predicted to them, rather discouraged. "Correct yourselves, educate yourselves, do you hear me? Perhaps you're all already dead?" Silence, breakdown. Silence and breakdown. I'd buried myself.»

Salom thought about it and after a moment resumed the anecdote.

«I'm happy now. How did I pull myself out of it? It's very simple. One day I fell in the middle of a crowded street, beaten down, frayed, dead of hunger. Crisant casually passed by, picked me up, and we talked.

"You're mistaken," he said to me. "You won't get anywhere with towns and men, you won't improve them in the slightest if you reproach their defects, defects already well known to all. On the other hand, they never end up knowing what positive qualities they have. If you show these to them, they will end up thanking you for it."

»Little by little, with circumspection, Crisant made manifest to me his doctrine, a doctrine which I followed to the letter. And I succeeded, as you all can see. Don't you know Crisant's theory? It's as amazing as it is simple.» «Wait,» the impatient Tomeu interrupted. «First say what you did to free yourself from being the redeemer.» «Who, me? Well, I was a lawyer. And in my spare time, as a distraction, a ventriloquist,» laughed the happy Salom. And then he went on to expound to us Crisant's theory.

# Crisant's Theory

Crisant Baptista Mestres—an eloquent man, with a medical degree and a love for *belles lettres* and philosophical digression, things they say are very entertaining hobbies—never had the need to work for a living when, all of a sudden, he lost his whole rich inheritance. «Crisant, dear, there's no bread in the house,» said his loving wife. «Let me get oriented, Laudelina,» commanded Crisant. «Alright,» he said at last. «We will go far, I promise you.» «Look at how we scarcely have any bread,» Laudelina began again. «Think pure thoughts, you know? My theory,» asserted Crisant, completely satisfied. «Fine, but what will we do to get bread?» his wife insisted. «Nothing more than think pure thoughts,» Crisant interrupted. «It's an infallible secret for prospering, girl. Ah, what a brain I have, what a man I am, among the best! You'll see the results in no time!» Crisant promised with great optimism. «Thinking pure thoughts: a method for conserving the body's health, combating all sickness, and extending life. Office: Dr. Crisant B. Mestres, Galatea 15,» was spread throughout the country.

«Think pure thoughts. You are intelligent, young friend!» he said to his first client. «Think pure thoughts and you will get better.» «What did he tell you, what did he prescribe for you?» people asked the first to try the new system. «We didn't talk about prescriptions, but on the other hand he told me some really useful things.» «That's it, he's a psychiatrist,» they said indecisively, and ran to Carrer de Galatea, number fifteen, to find out. «Come in, gentlemen, come in,» welcomed Crisant. «I'll get to you all very soon. What a noble head you have: think pure thoughts,» he said to one. «You are rich and, what's more, you know it, I know you know it. You deserve a fortune, and anyone who'd pull something against you would be committing a monstrous mistake. Think pure thoughts,» he advised another. «What a looker you are! No, no: looker, with an l, and I'm not from Valls; think pure thoughts,"» he said, enraptured, to a third. «What a nice man. And he's put everything in its place for me. He's a thaumaturge,» the flattered people said. «Oh, master Mestres!» they fawned. «You all are the best,» Crisant said. «So, do we have bread in the house now?» he asked his wife. «We'll never finish it, dear,» Laudelina responded enthusiastically. «You're the one who's really the best.» «Think pure thoughts,» Crisant reminded her. «Doing that is enough,» Laudelina very happily agreed. And the sick always filled the office on Galatea, 15, and all hastened to think pure thoughts, sustained by the small conviction of being the best. «I'm the best, no, doctor?» asked the old man Tobies Comes, spoiled by earthly goods. «I'm the best—no, doctor?» asked Count Trinitat Castellfollit, in those heady days the country's preeminent moneybag. «You're the best,» Crisant confirmed separately to Tobies and to the count. «You just have to think pure thoughts.» «Hurrah!» exulted those two incorruptible cavaliers and the legion that followed them. «Long live Psychopathic Crisant!» And everyone privately rejoiced at the sweet novelty, the evangelism of Crisant. «I am the best, I am the best,» the elderly Tobies hummed as he dressed before a mirror. And boom! he fell to the floor, as though struck by lightning, and made his debut as a cadaver. «Crisant, my elderly relative Tobies had a sudden ache, and now he's colder and stiffer than an Englishman, and he had the same illness that I had,» Count Castellfollit, who was above all considered a humorist, now stiff with fright, revealed quickly. «Don't take it that way, dear Count. They were quite different cases, yours and that of Tobies. Between us, I wasn't ever able to get the deceased to think pure thoughts. Tobies Comes was never one of the best. But our dear Castellfollit on the other hand, yes, and the best among the best,» Crisant said, calming him. «Thank you, thank you,» the count wept, euphoric. «Ask of me anything you want,» Crisant said. «I want nothing but to do good: I am a modest man,» Crisant said. «I am taking care of you. You are a soul that would obtain beatitude ahead of time. If we, your friends, didn't watch out for you, God protect us. No, we won't leave off, by no means, not until you sit, at the very least, among the immortals—for example in the Acadèmia de la Llengua,» answered the all-powerful Trinitat. «No, no, please,» Crisant, with a modest perfection, stammered. «Enough, silence: make this sacrifice for me,» requested the count. And Crisant was made an academician—one of his life's most hidden dreams—and adviser of the Banc Nacional, member of Parliament, president of the Board of Barefoot Indians, and professor of Characterological Graphology at the University, where he was suddenly surrounded by many disciples, among them the favorites Amaranta, Pupú Alosa, Ludovicus Baronet, Maria Victòria Prou, Mimí Pitosporos, and two or three silent, affected people who formed a closed, hermetic, circle; the circle of Crisant's orthodox doctrine. «We love him!» they said at the sight of themselves in such a highly eminent group. «You're all the best,» Crisant meted out in intimate settings. And he spread praise among his apostles. «What beautiful hands you have, Amaranta! And you, Alosa, the manner in which you move yours! And, you, Baronet, what beautiful silence! Silence is the best trait there is, because it allows pure thoughts to be expressed. And you all,» he said to the two or three affected people left, «you all are also the best, because you admire me and you admire so purely your companions.» «Glory be to Crisant!» the country exalted. And they offered him, in homage, a five-thousand-place meal. «Thank you, ladies and gentlemen,» Crisant began when it was his turn to deliver a speech. «Thank you for this bounteous downpour descending upon my head.» «A poet, goodness me, a poet! Thaumaturge, financier, academician, patron, and now poet,» the throng cried. «And master above all. He loves his pupils, he stimulates them, he helps them, he knows them, and then there's this school of great clinicians that he's created! What did you all tell me about Baronet's silence, Amaranta's hands, Alosa's gestures, Mimí's talks, or Victòria's tender spirit?» «You can count on this: they are great clinicians,» the public acknowledged. «I already know, dear Professor, about your great day yesterday," the Princess Bijou Fontrodona said the day after the event. «*N'est-ce pas, maman?*» «*Oui, ma fille, une journée tout à fait historique,*» the broken-down duchess, Stephana Martin, swallowing a yawn, agreed. «Surely I was needed there, being the country's only princess,» Bijou added. «And the best,» interrupted, gallantly, the great man. «You are adorable,» the Princess said, utterly pleased. «But I was not able to attend, due, as you will already have figured, to my husband, the Prince.» «Yes, of course, the Prince,» Crisant said. Then all three of them sighed. «And what are you thinking to do now, what projects do you have?» Bijou inquired. «Just a book,» the great man said, with an air of confidentiality. «A book in which you will no doubt express your curative theory, how fantastic,» the kind Princess said. «Yes, and moreover, a type of confession, an autobiography. For, ladies, I will reveal my hidden tragedy. In reality I am neither a clinician, nor a financier, nor a patron of barefoot Indians, an academic nor a poet. I am a philosopher. As a young man I followed the teachings of Efrem Pedagog, a sublime genius as far as I am concerned, and Efrem considered me the best of his pupils. I owe my whole doctrine to him. Life and circumstance took over afterward, and no one saw the philosopher in me, when in fact I am nothing other than a philosopher, or a failure: and there you have what I want to tell in my book.» «Really? A philosopher?» commented Bijou, with a bit of frost in her voice. But she quickly recovered. «You are terrible, Crisant! A philosopher. A failure . . . Your ambition has no limits, dear friend.» Everyone laughed, and Crisant's ears turned deep red from the psychological collapse. «Following a train of thought,» the Duchess said when everything calmed down. «I would like to ask you a favor, Crisant: nothing major, a little obligation. It is about Melània . . .

an old pupil of yours.» «Melània, Melània . . . » Crisant, trying to recall her, said. «Ah, yes, a Melània attended my lectures for three straight years. Not another word, Duchess, I implore you. Melània was intolerable. She never accepted my theory; she slandered it, only thinking of herself, and I find these flights of freedom unpleasant. Melània did not belong, to put it this way, in the category of the best,» Crisant explained. «Request of me, on the other hand, anything you may want done for Mimí or for Baronet, or for the good of Amaranta, or Alosa, or Victòria.»

# Introduction to the Study of a Small Giraffe

«You haven't heard?» asked Emma Raquel Baladre. «A little giraffe was born in our zoological park.» «When?» asked diligent voices. «Today at dawn,» Emma clarified, pleased by our attention. «Our zoo can rival the best in the world now. Actually, it's among the most important. Do you all know what it means that a giraffe was born in our city, in our climate? The treatment that had to go into the long gestation period, the discretion, the interest. Ah, our modest little zoo! People, I'm telling you: we don't have to be jealous, in this respect, of any other in the world,» perorated the renowned patriot Carranza i Brofegat. «Have you ever tended to any part of a giraffe?» Tomeu asked him. «No, but that doesn't mean I don't know what I'm talking about,» responded Carranza. «Ah, if you could all see the giraffe!» continued Emma Raquel Baladre. «So precious, so light, so little!» «It will always be bigger than a wolf-dog,» Tomeu pointed out, not being one who easily developed a soft spot for animals. «Yeah, man, the same for you,» Emma protested, slightly indignant. But she soon calmed down. «This morning, when I heard the news, I went to see it with my niece,» she continued. «She was so enthusiastic! And she wasn't scared at all.» «How old is she?» inquired those good souls Clàudia and Melània. «Not yet three,» Emma said. «The little thing!» Clàudia and Melània said. «It's been a while since we've seen her. You have to take us to her.» «It will be my pleasure,» Emma said. «Thank you,» Clàudia and Melània, ever good girls, said. «And you say the giraffe didn't scare her?» «Not at all; they even became friends. She cried out to it and the giraffe came to her as though it had known her all its life. The parent giraffes ambled backwards, very pompously, satisfied with their paternity. It was moving.» «Listen,» screamed Justi Petri, upon entering. «There's just been a new run-in between the troops and the extremists. I saw three or four soldiers with my own eyes laid out on the ground with shrapnel . . . Bloodcurdling!» «I don't feel bad for them, I just don't,» responded Emma Raquel Baladre, who was, during that period, a pioneer in those revolutionary ideas—ideas as full of hypocrisy as firm gravitas—that flourish today. «Four or five? It should have been more!» «Why?» Tomeu asked: «I have to enlist, and you well know it, some time in the near future. What would you say if I were one of the dead?» «Don't come to me now with complications,» Emma cut him off. «All I know is that gunning down lots of people, when they're your people, is abominable.» «But what do you want those boys to do? They're under orders, they can't do anything else,» Tomeu said. «Disobey,» Emma didactically offered. «They would shoot them on the spot for insubordination,» Tomeu countered, irritated. «Well, they would then win my complete respect,» Emma granted. «Right, but I'm not interested in that; it's the same stuff every day. We were talking, Petri, when you arrived, of real news: a little giraffe was born in our zoo.» «I'm surprised,» Petri confessed. And the conversation stretched on, with renewed drive. «The little giraffe died last night, Emma,» Melània said the following day. «Don't any of you talk to me about it! I was having breakfast when I found out and I couldn't put down another bite,» Emma lamented. «And what did it die of?» the patriot Carranza asked. «There are multiple stories, as you'll see. Some say that her mother, while asleep, crushed her. Others that it was the brutal jealousy of the father. Others, perhaps the closest to getting it right, said that it was due to complications from the birth. The thing is that it's dead. The mother is going to suffer badly, poor thing! Without a doubt they'll reduce its food. Because they feed it. Just think: besides the foliage, an entire bucket a day of milk to make it strong during lactation.» «I've had enough of giraffes!» Tomeu suddenly cried. «I've had enough of them! Thank goodness it's squashed.» «Heartless jackass!» Emma shot out. «You deserve . . . » «Guys!» our Justi Petri, bursting in on us, said. «The funeral for the fallen soldiers from yesterday is passing by now. Attending it . . . » «Poor giraffe!» melancholic Emma Raquel Baladre remembered. «Our modest zoo didn't have to be jealous, in that respect, of any other in the world!» added, quite measuredly, the renowned patriot Carranza i Brofegat.

# Topic

«A machine,» I explained once, «caught my friend Eleuteri while he was working» (during his short life he did nothing else) «and cut off his right femur. They say Eleuteri let out three or four extremely sharp cries. That he sprawled out on the floor, soaked in an expanding pool of blood. Some collapsed at the sight of him, others went to find help. The doctor showed up and gave many useless orders. Eleuteri was moved to an improvised ambulance, and they went off in search of an undiscoverable cure. Once his body had been well studied, they finally decided to carry him home to his mother. Folks piled up at the door, making much racket.

"What's this, what happened?" the old woman asked.

"Ok, don't get frightened. Eleuteri, at work . . .," began the tragic heart.

"He's dead!" the old woman shrieked.

"Yes, it's true; you had to be told," admitted the *coreuta*, a neighbor with the tested mettle ideal for these situations.

"I want to go where my son is, I want to see him," bellowed the unfortunate woman.

"Marieta, calm yourself, woman, you'll get yourself worked up," prophesied the kind souls. But the mother made headway and embraced her son's remains.

"How white!" everyone weighed in at the sight of him rigid on the bed. "Of course. He doesn't have even a drop of blood left in his veins. How did it happen? It hasn't sunk in."

»There were multiple stories of what had happened, and none of them were satisfactory. The cadaver meanwhile had a smile on its thin lips. The horrified, agonized grimace gone, his peaceful features reminded his mother of the boy's infancy, a world unto itself. Poor, little Eleuteri—so quiet and insignificant in life—had grown up, controlling this moment with supreme hierarchical power. Everyone revered the noble, marble man, the splash so new in the silence.

"Is the body all mangled?" the heart continued.

"No, and after a little bit of work by the doctor, sewing him up, you all wouldn't even know it. A deep gash on the right leg and that's it."

"He barely suffered while it was happening, surely," the doctor responded, swelling with pride from the praise. "The impact was so utterly violent that his sensory functions shut themselves off."

"He was my son," Marieta panted.

»Rows of solicitous witches mobilized and returned with orange blossom water, lime blossom tea, and piping hot tisanes.

"Drink it, Marieta."

"This woman won't be able to handle it, as delicate as she is, and maybe it would be for the best."

»Others opined that that wouldn't be the case, because who then would pray for poor Eleuteri? And they surrounded Marieta, they massaged her, joined her in wailing out her pain, each wanting to be the first to give thanks and praise. All of the women thought: "If it were to have been my boy at home!" And they terrified themselves, they wanted to distance the portent, and they hugged Marieta when it was their turn—and God willing, no one else's—to be in that, the bitterest of roles.

»The brother and fiancée of the deceased, having been urgently told, arrived. The brother was married, had a family, and for this reason he was immediately shut out from the front line of the grieving. The fiancée, on the other hand—poor girl!

"Almost a widow."

"You said it. They were getting married within the month, in November!"

»The upheaval of Nepomucè Garrigosa, Eleuteri's boss, was far more telling. He'd loved Eleuteri like a son, so much so that he'd taken him on as his apprentice! Eleuteri was so honorable, so good, and could do anything, and was so humble, so very prudent, and satisfied with little: he contented himself with a fifth of the salary he deserved.

"This is the first displeasure he's ever caused me. He had my complete confidence, I didn't even give him orders anymore, because he knew his obligations and never stopped working. If he had to work fifteen, twenty hours? He did it like that. And now this stupid, inexplicable death. I loved him like a son, I tell you, Marieta. The lady of the house didn't dare come, forgive her. You're in mourning, no? None of you would be able to keep up with her, she's even made herself sick."

»The tender discussion provoked spectacular weeping. What else? Eleuteri was watched over the entire night, and the following day the entire town accompanied him to the cemetery.

"The boy was insured, Marieta. With the new laws in place you'll receive at least fifty bucks, which is always a consolation. And don't you worry about the burial and the services, that's all on me. And what's more, here you have the wages for the week that poor Eleuteri didn't get to complete. Are you happy?"

»Mechanically, Marieta said *Yes*, and the boss left to calm his sick wife and he never went, nor did he ever have to go, by the house of the poor woman again.

"You're receiving fifty-thousand *pessetes*, serious money, in compensation; I'm sure of it," her neighbor the choralist assured her.

»Marieta earned a pension of thirty-nine *pessetes* a month[8], as the law demands, but folks envied her for the other, illusory amount. And everyone, excluding his mother, forgot about their friend Eleuteri.»

«Well, yes, the topic of the honorable worker, of the usually sensible boss, and the mother in misery,» Pulcre Trompel·li, who was listening to me, said. «Follow my advice: don't talk about Eleuteri any more. *Hélas, hélas, la bêtise humaine!*» whistled the clean-as-a-whistle Pulcre. And I responded immediately to that intelligent invitation to return to my senses. «Since Pulcre is correct, I have to bid you a final adieu, honorable, kind-hearted, hard-working

---

8   In the currency pre-dating our war. In order to obtain satisfactory biceps from today's social provisions, the reader ought, perhaps, to resort to—at least!—the weight and gymnastic strength of a potent zero. Or two. –S.E.

Eleuteri, beloved friend,» I thought. «I have to not talk about you, because you're a topic. But do you remember how we ran soaked in sun, drenched in sweat, chasing each other through streams, across fields of reeds, toward the beach? The whole group of us ran without taking a breath, drenched in sweat. And after, much later, you sprawled in your own blood, and now the earth covers you, and I won't talk about you any more, sorry, because Pulcre Trompel·li said you're a topic. And you know what? You wouldn't understand, but Pulcre is right. And it's terrible for me that Pulcre is right, my honorable, kind-hearted, hard-working, beloved Eleuteri.»

# The Subordinates

«Believe me, I am sorry,» the Director said, offering his condolences while lighting a fat Havana. «You're all receiving proof of my concern, my friends. I have the best opinion of you all.» «Thank you!» the subordinates said, down to the last. «But I can't do anything about this,» continued the Director. «I haven't been left any wiggle room to work with in this situation. Our Foundation depends, as you all know, on the State—this bankrupt, all-consuming State. Once we've achieved independence . . . » he added, lowering his voice. The subordinates made sufficient gestures of comprehension, immediately entering into the conspiracy. «Once we've achieved independence,» the Director continued, «these enormous abuses will not happen.» «Are you sure about that?» asked the wildly impatient secretary Teresiana Cacao. «Uf, *filla*, what questions!» the patriotic Director said. «Uf, what questions, co-worker Cacao!» psalmed like a choir the subordinates. «Let's celebrate the triumph of the cause in advance. Here you go!» the Director said. And he poured out, in measured amounts, generous glasses of wine. «Thank you!» said the subordinate choir, reverently. «To-the-health-of-our-Director!» they toasted, rhythmically. «Good,» the Center of Attention said when everyone had had a drink. «You have me forever, friends, at your disposal . . . » Everyone understood that the conversation was over. «So,» poor nervous, heretical Cacao said, «we're not going to receive the months' wages that they rightfully owe us?» «Girl!» her oldest co-workers warned. «Were you not listening?» the Director said very severely. «Ah—and I, little lady, prevent you from suffering any important distractions while at work. I dare to hope that you'll keep that in mind in the future.» Cacao turned whiter than she already was: a championship white. «I feel the delay; believe me. This State!» the Director said sarcastically. «You'll end up being paid, doubter! Good thing it's just about summer, though. You'll deal better with the wait. You know the popular saying.» «*A-l'estiu-tota-cuca-viu*,»[9] the subordinates recited in good spirits. The Director laughed. «Magnificent. Good humor. I like it. Well, see you in October, when we'll talk about this again. You deserve from me, ladies and gentleman, the best of opinions.» And he left, savoring his fat Havana. Within a minute his car, with its sounds of optimism, was off in the distance. «Now what will we do?» the subordinates, on their own again, asked a row of imperious mouths. «What are the Director's concepts going to give me? I make fifty bucks a month, I don't have any other source of income, and I have to support six kids, my wife, and, as extra weight, my mother-in-law!» exclaimed Benedicte

9   In essence, that during the summer it is relatively easy to be healthy and well fed. –RrP

Battistini. «And now they're proposing to squeeze me out of my salary. Swindlers!» Teresiana Cacao's sister had had an operation. They were orphans, they lived alone, and they were eating what little rations they had. No one anywhere else would want the senior member of the group, Verònica Marfà, she was too old. Anselm Lloveteres had a degenerate liver and every summer he patched himself up at a health retreat. But even though he needed to go there now more than ever, how could he leave the city if he didn't have a cent? And Baldomeret Moixí's big son, so tall and thin, half-consumptive, he needed mountain air even more than the bread he wasn't eating. And Querubí Torros, and Camil·la Misser, and Mitzi Santacana, and Paula Forns, and Òscar Tàpies, and Semproni Maians, and all the rest, with so many obligations, without savings or other options. «Meanwhile, that rascal of a Director rides around fine in a car, smoking Havanas, and he doesn't feel a hit from five bucks or a thousand *pessetes*. It's the State, he says. Hmpf, if the Director wanted it . . . !» the subordinates said, each in his or her own way. «I've been an employee here for fifty years and this has never happened to me before,» complained Verònica. «I have six kids, a wife, and an extra weight called my mother-in-law,» Benedicte Battistini repeated. «What slice of my salary will I have to live from?» «My sister's operation used up what little ration we had for all the things we were dreaming of,» cried the nervous Teresiana Cacao. «My liver!» Anselm Lloveteres exclaimed. «Ahak, ahak,» Baldomeret Moixí's big son coughed. «I suggest,» the sporty and petite Mitzi Santacana enthused, «a street demonstration by all of us.» «I'd love to,» seconded the combative Semproni Maians. «That way the public would be aware of our problem.» «*Santa cristià!*»

the rest of them cried out against it. «Sure, so we can be dismissed when the Director comes back, as excited as he and the people behind him would be to do it.» «I'm very sad,» said senior member Verònica. Everyone wanted to march. «How did you all manage through the summer? Well, I hope,» the Director said when October arrived. «Moixí, that poor boy, died; who'd have imagined it! I found out about it while abroad. A shame. You, Lloveteres, you have to take care of your liver, dear friend. I'm noting with some satisfaction that the others are enjoying some enviably good health, enviably good.» «Thank you!» the subordinates said. «Regarding our affairs, it seems as though things are going well, but you'll all have to have a little more patience, no big deal, nothing more than two or three months. All in all, I'm very sorry, I am so pleased with all of you! Yes, you are excellent collaborators, and I have, believe me, the best opinion of you all.» «Thank you!» psalmed the subordinate choir. «This won't get solved in one go while our country . . . Let's drink, because our country . . . » added the Director under his breath. And he lit a fat Havana and shared with each of them a highly scrutinized glass of liberation wine. «Thank you!» sang the subordinates, complicit in gesture and tone. «So, Mr. Director, we're not going to get paid now either?» suddenly shrieked the poor little nervous, heretical secretary Cacao. «Miss Cacao!» censured the Director, with stern seriousness. «Co-worker Cacao! But, my God, co-worker Cacao!» the subordinates, unanimously, warned.

# Ghettos

A hard slap on the back stopped me as I was crossing the street.

«I wasn't expecting to see you here.»

And suddenly, intimate details about those eternal themes: money and women. And the intimate details blended with manifestations of joy. My friend was robust and accustomed to eating a lot. During his golden era all sorts of feminine hearts sighed in his wake, with more or less interest, according to what could be gained.

«He causes quite the commotion,» folks said with envy.

Later, rheumatic, married with children, the poor guy didn't even provoke pity. Life is like that.

But on that day he still spoke to me effusively.

«I tell you, it's worth the trouble.»

He drew up a plan:

«With these ladies right here. What do you think?»

He resumed:

«You're a piece of work, man. No doubt about it. Come with me.»

Down narrow streets, we soon lost ourselves among the shrieks of children and the voices of street vendors selling peanuts. Dusk. Swelter. Calmness glided above Lavínia. Dust, idleness, bust-ups, blasphemies. From time to time a shower of trash fell from the terraces. Dogs threw themselves onto the waste and fought over every crust they found in the filth. A man passed, his face covered by a mask of pus. From the doorways, women called out to us.

«You want dinner? We can spend some time together.»

We entered a tavern. A man came out from behind the bar to greet us; a plump, bent-legged man with a hunchback and a shrill voice. He introduced himself to us in a long, thin room, full of tables with stained cloths. The remains of some thirty castaways sought refuge there. Roar, the stench of extremely cheap tobacco, the squeak of knives on the cartilage of dead meat recommended on a chalkboard with the highest possible praise, the rhythm of sips. Each dish had to be paid for in advance. No one trusted the person beside him. A black man, tall as Saint Peter, stirred his thick broth. He spilled it. His stirring had picked up speed and caused a motion in the stew he couldn't stop; it coaxed a groan out of him. But then he had a change of heart and joyously licked up the stew-soaked spots. Meanwhile, a freckled girl entered accompanied by a louse. The man asked her for more money. She resisted. Without a sound, the thug began roughing her up. Everyone watched indifferently.

«That fly will get tired at some point, I'm telling you,» the black man said, fraternizing during a pause in his hunt for the stew. And, convinced, he scratched an ear.

«Ready?»

We left, not very full, though we'd been there a while. We turned a corner and my friend pointed out an electric sign for a music hall.

«Here.»

Some couples swayed with great difficulty and pain, holed away in that reduced space. Blanched faces, fatigued glances. And sweat. A sticky, greasy sweat. A waitress sat with us, though she was soon called away. When she came back she was breathing heavily.

«Everything for four cents. And it's still good,» she said. Some inverts passed by, making a huge fuss as they did, and the woman named them all for us: the one with the plucked eyebrows was the Crazy Virgin; and the one with the body of a snake and the fleshy lips, Skin and Bones. And Pitoperume, with the white flannel pants and mallow-colored silk shirt, like a farmwoman's dream blouse debuted beneath the awning of a village fair. And Little Pigeon, a really fat woman with enormous haunches, and Golden Pheasant, and the Lion, and Iris and his lover, Chrysanthemum, with bracelets, blonde hair, and bangs. With a woman's scorn the waitress detailed the works and miracles of that troupe.

«And this is where they run down their prey—the cretins.»

The ragtag band struck up a Charleston. Cymbals, bass drum, *violinassa*. Heads, bellies, legs waved about.

«That's her!» my friend suddenly screamed. «Eh, what do you think, was I exaggerating?»

And he got up to reunite himself with his Aphrodite: a stupid, old, and very ugly goose.

«And if it's Josep Sereno!» I protested.

He didn't hear me.

«I'm leaving,» I told the haze.

Strange love absorbed him. I left.

«How exciting!» said Pura Yerovi, a little woman married not long ago. «I've never been to Lavínia's ghettos. You have to take me there, I want to have a good time,» she demanded of her husband. «And you will all accompany us.»

«No,» I responded sharply. «I have neither the interest nor can I be bothered to set foot in that faithful but terrible cliché, ever again.»

«This is a city of perfect beauty, the admiration of all the land,» said erudite and stupid Salom, with no exactitude at all.

# The Literary Circle

Once the lists of pharaohs had been recited by heart, Tianet, the prodigy, listed the Roman emperors, the devout Christian kings of France, the charming kings of England, and all the crowned miseries of Spain.

«The dynastic problems of the kingdom of Leon have always puzzled me,» the tidy and talkative apothecary observed as Tianet listened. At a sign from his father the boy repeated the familiar complications of the dynasties of Leon.

«Is it clearer to you now?» the father asked.

«Definitely. Quite clear,» agreed the apothecary.

And he kept himself from opening his naïve mouth again, while from the phenomenon's own rolled illustrious names, evoked by an infallible memory—without a hint of dyspnea—abundant with dates and complementary allusions. The boy carried out his task under the satisfied gaze of his father: it had cost him a pretty penny or two, but had brought them glory. On the other hand, his wife disapproved of the education that they were giving the adolescent. Culture causes you to lose your soul, it dries out the brain. Had he, her husband, needed it to become rich? Hearing this argument angered the father, and he adopted the most tearful tone in his repertory. He didn't want the boy to have as miserable a life as his! Then the members of the circle praised, unanimously, his work ethic, his business acumen, the decency of that good father. His wife agreed with them, and at last the boy took up the strain as well. And they all stoned him with great applause.

«The boy will go far,» the apothecary assured. The father accepted it.

«What he has to be is a good boy,» his mother desired. «He can't let all of these things go to his head!»

Everyone protested against this possibility. With the memory that the little boy had! The father, smiling, qualified that observation.

«Well, it's not all memory, either. There's a little bit of talent, too, it has to be said.»

«Of course, that too!» conceded the members of the circle.

That wrapped up, the doctor broached the topic, particularly red-hot in Konilòsia in those days, of Proust.

«Oh, Proust, Proust!» the doctor summarized, his eyes rolling back into his head with ecstasy.

«Oh, Proust, Proust!» the other members of the circle exulted in solidarity.

«I know nothing of this man,» the father, perplexed and full of candor, confessed.

«Neither do I,» said the boy, turning red.

«Boy!» his progenitor chastised, indignant.

«You're not being fair,» the doctor eased in to say. «He's too young to be reading Proust.»

«He's too young to be reading Proust,» confirmed the apothecary. «At his age I still hadn't read him.»

It was the closing stages of the third decade of this century. The apothecary was seventy-three years old. The phenomenon under discussion, fifteen. Now and again some jokes are best explained.

«Ah, that's what I thought!» said the father, calming down.

«My son,» groaned the mother. «And you want him to swallow these huge books? So that we'll grow apart.»

«Okay,» the father cut her off. «Tell me something about this Proust, doctor. Who was he?»

«Novelist,» clarified the doctor with some honest vacillation.

«That detail I knew,» the erudite boy, with his fillet of a voice, said.

«Ah, you knew that?» the father happily cried out. «Take heed, gentlemen, the boy already knew that detail. It's likely that he knows quite a bit about it! Let's hear.»

«I don't know anything more, papa,» the boy assured him.

«Poor you, if you have to swallow this filth.»

«That's enough, woman,» ordered the husband. «Okay, talk to us for a while about Proust, Doctor,» he demanded. «In order to round off my boy's concept of him.»

«Well yes, a novelist,» began the practitioner, stammering and choking. «A great literary creator, almost incomparable. And an acute psychological analyst. Oh, Proust, Proust!»

«He's embellishing,» commented the father. «I'm getting situated.»

«A type of modern Voltaire,» the apothecary, who was himself trying to become a type of modern Voltaire, said.

«Ha, ha, ha!» everyone, in on the joke, laughed. And they held back on the diabolic stuff.

«They've already said enough indecencies,» deplored the mother. «Tianet, child, go to bed right now. What's more, tomorrow you have your comedy in the garden of five trees, and you have to rest.»

«I'm on my way, mama,» he said reluctantly. «I knew those details, too,» the adolescent whispered in his father's ear.

«You're quite modest. Why did you keep quiet about it?» scolded the fascinated father.

«Because the doctor is a specialist in it,» the boy said prudently.

«You're quite modest,» the father hugged him. «But I don't tolerate timidity; not that. Tianet knew the particulars,» he shared with his intimate acquaintances.

«Ah!» all the members of the circle ambiguously filtered out.

«Good night,» said the boy, and the other members of the circle, their expressions dim, reciprocated.

«And what will you be performing tomorrow in the garden of five trees?» the doctor asked.

«One of Salom's impromptu productions about a queen from the Bible,» the father said. «In it the boy sings some names that no one but he could have learned. That Salom,» he added, «is probably a wise man, I won't deny that, but I don't trust him.»

«They say he's a Jew,» the apothecary said indignantly.

«Everyone who's doing well is. As much as he's given me, I don't trust him,» the father responded. And next they drifted happily into politics. The doctor took the reins. And after, having been schooled, the other members of the circle called it a night.

«See you tomorrow,» they said to one another.

«That little boy will have learned his lesson comfortably,» the doctor said to the apothecary once they were outside.

«Me too,» the apothecary, agreeing whole-heartedly, added. «He's even capable of having read Proust. I wouldn't risk it, I swear.»

«It is to be feared. My dissertation sufficiently ruined me,» the doctor regretted. «And it would be indecorous at his age.»

«Watch out for the boy, he's scaring me,» the woman said to her husband, now that they were alone. «Look, he's very young, and you two have some conversations . . . I don't follow it, poor me, but I'm telling you . . . And he works so much that it frightens me. It can't be. He can't fall sick on us.»

«Nonsense. He's strong as an oak!» the father optimistically laughed. «May he study, may he study. You'll see your son, you'll see: he's going to end up a tenured professor.»

«In order to earn the salary of a cop, a cap-maker, a hot-air-balloon captain,» the mother lamented, addicted by instinct to the puzzles provided by statistics.

«And for whom have I migrated and pined away?» toyed the obese, rotund, and metaphoric father. «I'll be diligent in giving him my support.»

Meanwhile, upstairs, the boy dreamed of the normal perils, a bicycle to mess around on, and Emília, who had incredible legs, at his side. And, already lodged in the dream, he felt a pair of eyes staring fixedly at him. Under the orders of those eyes he went through a list of names just as he'd learned them: Mehuman, Bizta, Harbona, Hegai, Bigtan, Teres. Those eyes examined him as though he were already dead and, at the same time, as though they only proposed to save the everlastingness of a moment. Abagta, Atac, Zetar, Carcas. They were a pair of eyes that, through the alembics of subtle reason, respected everyone, without either loving or hating, with a cold sadness, and almost never appreciated anyone, as though they contemplated things from a past cloaked in mist, as though they spied from a remote future. And a pair of long hands removed the puppet, the marionette, from a dark box, and slipped it on like a glove, or moved it around with invisible strings, moved it for a pathetic and superfluous instant, and immediately put it away again with the other dolls, an anonymous mix. Memucan, Carsena, Aman, Sethar, Admata. But the eyes weren't outside of time, eternal—they were mortal, like the show. Trained, cautious, strange, distanced, tired, without any answer to any question. Mortal. The profound acceptance of an ineluctable law perhaps dignified them, and perhaps they attempted from that law to justify their characters, understanding themselves a little in their characters. Tarsis, Meres, Marsena. Though how would the adolescent Tianet rummage and toil in the chaos? The eyes moved away from him, erasing him, and the bicycle and Emília's legs again filled all his sleep. Keep in mind, keep in mind, that those imaginings would transitorily weaken the memory, and Tianet had to keep his own paired off and prompt for today's show in the garden of five trees: Forsandata, Dalfon, Asfata. And Forata, Ahalia, Aridata. And Farmasta, Arisai, Aridai. And Vaizata.

# The Conversion and Death of Quim Federal

## I

Quim Federal, lying atop a crumpled straw mattress, prophesized that the point of no return had arrived, and told Rossenda, erect and disheveled before him. The conversation, in the disorder of the bedroom, strained into screaming.

«Ai, I'm dying, Rossenda!»

«Your mother!»

«I'm telling you that I'm dying, love, that the same women won't touch me tomorrow.»

«Don't scare me; I'm in a delicate state and I can't take it.»

«I'm kicking the bucket.»

«Murderer!»

«Now this I don't get.»

«What's wrong with you, Federal? What's all this chitter-chatter for?»

«I swear to you, Rossenda, you're going to see me cooking sardines up there, not even fifty-three.»

«You're stealing from the faith, non-believer: you're close to ten times six, big baby; you know as much. And me, a teacher, getting old, dragged through that lack of an experience with Pinxo Arruga; wasted.»

«Now's not the time to exact revenge. Up there it thunders and nothing changes if there are three more or three less. The point is that my thunderclap has come. Ai, Rossenda, my belly!»

«Hold on tight, Quim. At least until one of the servers makes you a tisane. God forbid they should say that, because I mean nothing to you, you went to perdition without all the details taken care of.»

«Don't make fun, Rossenda, I'm trying to be brave.»

«Murderer. Here I am alone with you and you're getting on my nerves. Where does it hurt?»

«Here, Rossenda, in my belly. I already told you. Don't move me. The ghosts aren't here to soften the mattress.»

«Ai, Jesus, here comes the gibberish—now I know. Quim, try to breathe easy to the end, remember your good fortune, that this little adventuress has given you years and locks on your doors and skin with but few wrinkles. I'm not going to tell you to make use of it now, but I am going to tell you that you've acted like you're seven. Honestly, Quim, think about the fact that you're leaving me here in tears, yet not even a widow. What if we fix all the little details regarding our living arrangement? We just have to put it down in writing and everything will be for the better.»

«Ai, I'm dying!»

«Come on now, Quim, give me the pleasure of being able to legitimately dress like a widow in mourning.»

«Rossenda.»

«What?»

«It's called: "Please."»

«Please.»

«Shut your mouth and remember that you're dealing with Quim Federal.»

«Ai, mother, someone is working themselves to the bone, and all to show the shame of your final moments when I'm out on the street! Egotist, thief! Unlucky me!»

«No more of your lip. Do what you want as long as you shut up, witch.»

«That's better, and from your conscience. I'm going to go notify Father Apagallums.»

Rossenda left, and Federal, as a prologue to his final moments, wallowed in his bed.

# II

Upon leaving, Rossenda bumped into Ventura, the sacristan, who made her turn around and, on the way, informed her of the momentary absence of Father Apagallums: when he returned, he'd prepare Federal's filthy little soul. As the two of them entered the room, this was the sacristan's greeting:

«*Pax tecum*!»

«Out, out beetles. I'm a federalist for life.»

«I'm no beetle. Is it possible you don't recognize me—that I've slipped right through your memory? Quimet, you surprise me!»

«Ah, you're Ventura. Sacristan or not, boy, give me your hand. Good to see you, yes sir, friends are friends.»

Ventura, having re-established their old friendship, indicated Rossenda:

«Is she, shall we say, your concubine?»

«Technically, yes.»

«Uf, so inconsiderate, the two of you. I am a decent woman.»

«Take it down a notch, stop and calm yourself, girl. Don't you get it? Here: he simply asked me if you're getting any closer to being my wife.»

«Ah, thinking the worst, pardon me. I think this one never went to sewing school.»

«That's how I like it. Above all, that you don't fight. It's been months since I've seen you, Quim, but today my heart told me to come by, and here you have me. And so, how are things with you? Are you still abiding by your credo?»

«Yes, like always. You know how it goes: A dead bug's a free bug, and that's all she wrote.»

«You know you need me, blasphemer; I've already sniffed that out. I already see the signs, see you transformed, squashed suddenly flat as a decal, damned from head to toe in the thick sulfur of Hades. Repent. You still have time.»

«Now that's a Christian sermon,» said Rossenda. «If it didn't come at such a cost, I'd let out a little scream. Doesn't it move you, heretic, demon-son? Prepare yourself with the sacristan, so that when Father Apagallums arrives he can execute the blessing of union for us with, I hope, a quick benediction for two and a half *pessetes*, for when you go stiff, and I don't want to remove more than half of my black cloth.»

«Wicked, both of you. Coerce your consciences free. Let me go to the ground in peace.»

«Doing so little you'd end up fine, you dummy.»

«I don't believe in anything, Ventura. You, on the other hand, scoffed at the cause.»

«A feeling touched and softened me. I saved myself. If you prepare yourself now to be purged, I can accomplish the same for
you. You'll hit it in time.»

«Ventura, you're my friend, but if you get on my nerves I'm going to throw a fistful of mud at you.»

«Give yourself to God, you fool.»

«I'm paying dearly for it, but I don't believe in anything.»

«This man is not very Spanish. Son, good brother, repent.»

«Genius. I've never seen hide nor hair of Andebel:[10] how do you
expect me to believe in him? I'm standing firm. With a good dose
of terror, but firm.»

Federal's mouth filled with froth. The silhouettes of Rossenda
and the sacristan, frightening, lengthening in the half-light, were
reflected on the bedroom wall.

# III

Bam, bam, bam: a few knocks on the door. Rossenda opened it
and Pancraç, the cobbler from the same floor, came in.

«Excuse me. The woman just now told me that we're maybe not
doing too well.»

«Ai, Cobbler Pancraç, we're in the final moments.»

«In the final moments and condemned by God. The man wishes
to fester.»

«Ai, Jesus, Mary, and Joseph!»

---

10   A word for God in Caló, commonly referred to as the language of
gypsies, a mixed Romani and Romance language. –RrP

That pious exclamation birthed an idea in Ventura's imagination. He asked the cobbler:

«Do you have principles?»

«Come on now!»

«Excellent. I've thought up a serious piece of comedy to convert Federal. Would you dress up for me as the delegate Patopí? I invoke you, and you appear in the window. Work for you? For an orchid or two?»

Rossenda helped:

«Oh, yes, compatriot cobbler, let's have Father Apagallums find you ready when he arrives. And, also do me the favor of sending one of your *canalletes* to the rectory. If Father Apagallums is there. Hurry.»

Being a good fellow, Pancraç conceded:

«Well, I can't go to the tavern today anyway, as it's the first of May. I'll be right back.»

When he left Federal asked:

«What did Pancraç say?»

«Nothing, that he knows an unguent, and is going to look for it.»

«Ai, ai, I'm dying.»

«Convert, dummy, and cleanse yourself.»

«Don't come at me with more nonsense, sacristan; enough with the racket.»

«We're going over this in detail, Federal, which is my duty. Just now you affirmed that you've never seen a single sad thread of Andebel. If you were to have a peek at one—were it merely a modest representative—would you believe in Him?»

«Manú, if it were true, really true, you tell me!»

«Then I beg that Patopí consider my honor, and the great peril of this pigeon-shit of a soul. Show this inveterate your power and give me the strength to transmit without dilation your real imminence upon the balcony.»

«Ai, ai, don't make me laugh: I'm dying!»

Rossenda shrieked:

«Laugh? Look.»

The balcony opened with a din. A blast of light. The effigy of Patopí, silhouetted in the window. The messenger offered a blessing:

«Greetings.»

Scared, Quim Federal screamed:

«I'm trembling, I see, I believe, I want to make peace!»

«Wait for Father Apagallums, you fool; I have no authority.»

«I want the reconciliation to be open and out in public. Ai, sinner, federalist, so much nerve: impenitent, how many offenses! I don't know if I'll have time to look deep down inside myself and pour all of them out. And above all, one, Patopí: I've been having follow-ups with the wife of the cobbler from downstairs for more than thirty years.»

A huge bustle. Patopí swore:

«Fuck. And I had to dress up like Patopí to hear that?»

The timely, final convulsions of the moribund man in his bed. Everyone ran to him. Ventura checked out Federal, closed his eyes, and afterward said to Rossenda:

«I feel I should tell you, 'Senda, that God handled this better than we did.»

Rossenda moaned:

«Ai, and Father Apagallums hasn't come! Ai, what will happen to me, poor me? Alone and in mourning without getting a cent!»

«Calm yourself. You still look fine enough. Do you want to come with me and be a sacristan half the time, and the other half whatever?»

Rossenda calmed herself, suddenly, and accepted the deal:

«Ai, I'm very grateful!»

They hugged, and now the cobbler's grief burst wide:

«Ai, poor, poor me! Thirty years of being cuckolded by Federal. And I lived so happily, without suspecting a thing!»

The sacristan and Rossenda consoled him:

«The dullards are always the last to figure it out, that's well known, and on the other hand you've performed a work of mercy.»

Pancraç conceded:

«That I have.»

This was Ventura's profound final commentary:

«A mournful scene. We are no one.»

Pancraç growled:

«Thirty years! This is what I'll be remembered for, not for my skills as a cobbler, I swear.»

And he was about to cross the threshold. Charitable and snide, Ventura made a final wish on his behalf:

«Make sure you don't bump scatterbrained into the lintel now and smash your tottering noggin up there.»

The cobbler had already learned how to bellow with pride. And he left the abode with dignity and without any further damage. Already alone, Ventura and Rossenda went about dressing the stiff, and the popular and edifying fable ended there.

# English Quasi-Story of Athalia Spinster

*To Jaume Vidal Alcover, in homage to his great art as a writer.*

## I

They talked afterward, it's true, about Moore, Shelley, Dryden, and thirteen old Italian *maestri*, but their long conversation, full of interesting things, didn't blot out from Quildet's memory Athalia's first question:

«Have you ever been to England?»

And, martyr to the truth, Nogueres responded amid the most arduous of silences:

«No, never, but I should like to go there.»

It was truly an arduous silence. Until Maggie Brown finished nibbling her umpteenth toast of the afternoon. «I believe you to be quite unhappy, dear,» Athalia said. «This is my most intimate opinion,» Nogueres confessed. «But pretty Thalie, the fault is completely yours,» Pamela assured her. «You ought never to begin a chat about a theme of grammatical character.» «I share that opinion,» Melussina said. «Not all African gentlemen have been to England, although it is appropriately charming that they seem regretful for not having been.» Quildet coughed. Aretusa and Phoebe turned pale on hearing that and fled to wreathe their heads with white oleander. «Pre-Raphaelites!» the refined Pamela praised. «Shocking! Why did you cough?» Athalia, quite bothered, asked. Quildet reddened. «It is that Miss Melussina,» Nogueres said, stammering, «did me the honor of mistaking my place of birth.» «No matter,» Maggie said as she finished swallowing her toast. «On the other hand, she did call you *gentleman*.» Quildet, surrendering, lowered his head. And now the conversation drifted toward Bigordi and multiple aspects of English poetry. It finished just at sunset. «How beautiful, the dying sun today!» whispered Athalia. And she cried out to Aretusa and Phoebe to dance the Dance of Farewell. «Delicious!» Melussina said, applauding. «It is a love of rhythm.» «It is a love of rhythm,» sighed Maggie. «They have smashed the ineffability of the moment to pieces,» a regretful Athalia Spinster scolded. «Ah, Maggie!» Meanwhile, night imposed itself all around, and the bumblebees and mosquitoes freely crisscrossed the vast empire. «My dear legs!» Melussina lamented. And yet, despite it all, it was an intense hour of poetry. Aretusa and Phoebe had stopped dancing and now chased fireflies and other gentle extenuating circumstances of the dark. «The moon!» announced the little voices of the two girls. «The moon, the prune—or the gloom?» Athalia repeated suddenly; and questioning, just because. The barn owls began to gasp far off in the oak wood. «If it is permitted that I may say so, I'm scared,» declared the fragile Melussina. «The gasping of the nocturnal birds frightens me. It is, in a certain way, a bank-ruptcy of civilization.» And she went off toward the bath, attached to Pamela's hip. Then Maggie, in a very low voice, began to speak at great length about calid and disturbing deviations of feeling. To highlight these, she recited from a letter, in reality a fragment from one of her unpublished novels, which takes place in the most fruitful period of the Italian Renaissance. We would not think of depriving you of a taste of the wasted novelistic talents of Maggie Brown, who died, as the chord of her youth turned sour, not very long ago, of an excess of exquisite hydronium. It seems to us appropriate, we insist, to transcribe, translating with utter care and proper license, the letter that Maggie recited that memorable night to Lady Athalia Spinster and Quildet Nogueres.

## II

«Andreu, cardinal of the Santa Església Catòlica Romana, greeted the Lady Juliana, his wife,» Maggie sang. «Deliberate cacophony?» Lady Spinster, a master orthologer, asked. «Historico-onomastic rigor,» Maggie pointed out. «This prologue makes me happy,» Quildet said. «I see the cardinal as one of those painted by Raphael, with eyes set on returning to the *born*[11] of Lavínia and the entertaining hands of a poisoner.» «Silence!» interrupted Athalia. «Continue, Maggie.» «My thought, lady, so inclines itself toward

---

11    A designated area where medieval competitions between knights, such as jousts, were celebrated. The name of the present day Barcelona neighborhood El Born, among other areas in Catalunya, is derived directly from this word. –RrP

you, that I could not say whether, in fact, it is mine,» Maggie continued. «Memory of and desire for your presence fills all of my scant free time, and you, likewise, lady, soften all the harshness of my time at work.» «I find, in those emotional circumstances, that this highly eminent gentleman has chosen quite a modern lexicon. Would the Lady Juliana understand him?» observed Nogueres. «If you hinder Maggie so often, the sweet roundness of our moon is going to end up spoiled,» Athalia chided. The author continued her talk. «What have you done, lady, since we saw one another? Did you think at some point of our servant? Have you perhaps been ill? Tell me, even if it is but one word, remove me from the agony in which I live. You do not know how cruel this long wait is to me. Ovid expressed in a few elegant words this torment that I suffer: *"Res est solliciti plena timoris amor."* Be good, then, lady. Erase my fears and liberate me from this death, returning me to life with news of you.» Maggie ran out of air, and Quildet took advantage of the pause. «I don't know how the classics manage to transform familiar places into marble,» Quildet said admiringly. «They were stone-cutters,» Lady Spinster responded. «Come,» Maggie continued. «All the joy and all the pain of my life remains compressed in these two words: presence, absence. And I wish you near me. Judge me, then, as your separation from me is detestable to me.» «Daring, Miss Brown,» said Nogueres. «The following is even more so,» the novelist said. «In your last letter,» Maggie toiled again, «you mentioned my ignorance of many aspects of sin and regret. Refuse these ideas, I beg you, because there is no sin in beautiful things, and you are beauty itself. Love is a god, and one of its divine attributes is perfection. I assure you, as a cardinal and as a man devoted to you, that I have nothing sinful to point out to you in your conduct. What are you afraid of, that you separate yourself from me? Or perhaps it is that the friendship of an old man angers your splendorous youth. Come, come at once. I need you, I desire it. I demand it.» «Intense, vigorous, brave. Really,» enthused Athalia. «What do you think of it, Nogueres?» «Yes,» declared Quildet. «And more, Miss Maggie?» «Will you all excuse me, forgive my madness, but I do not care about anything in this world any longer, without you,» obeyed the author. «Live, live and love. The time for regrets is still far off for you, and you do not want to pierce the glory of your life with the sting of re-morse. Come, I implore you, and do not forget above all that, with or without shortcomings, you are always lovely. And since, as a man, I am weak and a slave to temptations, it is as a member— although unworthy—of our highly revered Senate that I absolve you of all fault.» «Enough, Maggie, enough!» cried out Athalia, agitated. «Your images weaken me profoundly. You shouldn't read the Freudians so much, dear.» Without adding even a single word, Maggie freed herself from her synthetic dress and headed, com-pletely nude, toward the nearby stream.

## III

There was noise and splashing about in the cold water. «What pu-rity of flesh, kissed by the pale star,» Athalia said. «Ohhh!» ad-mired Quildet. Silence reigned, disturbed only by the laughter of Aretusa and Phoebe, now bathing companions of slender Maggie. «This is an expression of near ritual unction,» added Athalia, «the water's virginity unsoiled by clothing. Oh, Franciscan Maggie! Oh, humble religious woman!» Quildet whistled an unfavorable tune between his teeth. But, against all reason, Thalie approved of it. «What a melody!» she said. «Is it from your land of hard sun? Oh, kiss me!» What could he do: Nogueres kissed her. «Well,» uttered Athalia. «I thank you for this experience.» And she also proceeded to undress. «Dear Lady Spinster, you see that I'm just an African,» Nogueres believed himself obliged to say. «You will not impose upon me any idealized performance, I dare hope, dear Lady.» «Alas! When I wanted to ask you your opinion about J. de Nazareth!» Athalia exclaimed. «I only know,» Nogueres responded «that religious feeling must be supported now, distinctly, and above science.» «Agreed,» agreed Athalia. «The formula is this: the really beautiful, etc., and whatever liberating type of syncretism to round things off.» Nogueres' eyes passed over Athalia's brown skin. «Ah, syncretism, Lady Spinster!» Quildet said. «I have always been partial to theories of syncretism.» And he bent down forcefully, more out of duty than willingness, to pick up Athalia, intending, altruistically, to carry her off to the brush of the oak wood with its barn owls. «No, not this, I'll scream,» the woman warned. Nogueres breathed: Athalia was heavy. «Are you condemning me to an idealized performance?» asked, with sweet reproach, Quildet, the hypocrite. «This is a vile subject, my dear,» Athalia attenuated. «Let us talk about other, more elevated things, it is preferable.» A Sandow[12] of silence stood between the two peo-

12   Eugen Sandow (1867–1925): Prussian bodybuilder and strongman, referred to as the "father of modern bodybuilding."

ple equally but oppositely affected. «A thinness of ideas has never, ever taken me for a victim; and I'm not just saying that. And now, on the other hand . . .» Athalia said bitterly. «Don't pay any attention to it, we all find ourselves there. I, myself . . .» consoled Nogueres. «Perhaps everything would work better if you were to get dressed,» he concluded, a bit bored. «Oh, I understand; thank you!» the middle-aged Athalia responded to an ambiguous Nogueres. And she dressed. The spring-like nakedness of Maggie and her companions continued to cut a profile in the moonlight. Athalia looked at the suspended Nogueres and gave it a shot. «A pedagogical conversation is probably the best therapy for an engrossed savage,» she said, subconsciously betrayed by the memory of a poster of the Methodist Missions. «How many times smaller is the moon than the Earth?» «Forty-nine,» Quildet, answered mechanically, hypnotized, spying off into the distance. The stubborn silence's dominance returned, but Athalia didn't lose heart. She searched her memory again, with application and honesty.

«Have you ever been to England?» inventive, she finally said with a flash of hope in her eyes.

The polite Nogueres suddenly reacted, in an unexpected way.

«No, never,» he bellowed. «But I should like to go there.»

And he fled quickly toward Maggie's unfurling beauty, Maggie the erudite novelist, nude and wet in the stream.

# Panets Walks His Head

«It has to be Olympian,» advised Efrem Pedagog, gesturing amply. «Olympian, which is to say, felt and understood with plenitude. Like me, debilitating modesty aside.» He coughed. «Is that you yet?» he then asked, with peremptory interest, Amadeu Panets who was listening to him. «Not really, I think, not yet,» Panets, an Alderian, confessed. «It has to be, young man,» said Pedagog severely. «And how?» Amadeu inquired. «Oh, it's really quite easy,» Efrem expounded. And he fell into meditation. Panets didn't insist. «Olympian, Olympian? I don't get it,» he said, having parted from the Master. And he went to consult Saurimonda, accredited health practitioner. «Breath or saliva?» were the given choices from firm commercial willfulness. «Cards,» chose Panets. «My set isn't that good. But whatever,» Saurimonda said. Shuffled. «In your case: head high,» Saurimonda read. «The cards have spoken.» Panets checked them. «Poor me, what a bother,» Panets complained. «Patience. You'll get used to it in no time,» Saurimonda mused. «Ok,» Panets interrupted. «When?» «Take your leave from here!»

Saurimonda disinterestedly said, with a laugh as fat and beneficent as a bishop. «Willfulness.» His will was bitter. «Ugh!» Saurimonda let out. But Panets was already gone. «And now what, Panets?» Amadeu asked himself on the way back home. «Head high? I mean, it has to get to Olympian proportions.» And he stretched out his head as best he could. «Stiff neck?» Semproniana asked with a caregiver's impulse. «Olympism,» Panets declared arrogantly. And he spoke at length all evening long about the satisfying fact of his being a mother's son like the one most so, and about the erudite subject of "one man, one vote." «Misery!» the sad and fecund Semproniana said. «Do you want a massage for your stiff neck?» There was a silence full of vacillations. «Yes, it hurts,» Panets accepted in defeat. But the following day he returned, well rested, to being stubborn about his head. «It's hard, but I have to get used to it,» Panets heartened himself by saying. And he left. «Hey, what do you think, Maestro?» Panets asked Efrem Pedagog after running into him. «Let's see? Well, well, well: a noble head this is,» Pedagog approved. «I predict in you a brave and authentic trend toward olympism.» «Yes!» «Carry on, young man,» Pedagog said. And they went their separate ways. That night there was no need for massages. «Panets, dear, don't be so hard-headed,» his wife said. «If this still . . . » «Better that you quiet yourself, Pronianeta,» Panets threatened. «I know what I'm doing to myself.» And months passed over his definitively surging head. «If this is olympism, it's easy,» Panets said when his sternocleidomastoid and adjacent muscles adequately toughened. «Long live olympism!» And he surrendered, within the inches he'd acquired, to the passion of feeling and understanding with plenitude. «I am a citizen,» Panets confessed to himself. «I'm an admired citizen, surely.» And his head climbed another inch. «Who's that with the imposing head?» the people asked. «That? Panets,» voices explained. «The head makes him seem important, a milestone-man. Introduce him to me,» people said. And Panets was presented. «He has a doctrine,» the people approved. «And it seems that his head knows all the best of what has been written, thought, or played over the centuries,» the people praised. «Perhaps I'm not just an admirable citizen,» Panets felt. And he wrote verses. And he triumphed. «The great poet of our land: Amadeu Panets,» one critic wrote, «knows how to conjugate the complexity of sounds within skillful architecture, at the same time giving, if he must, the simple note of words vertically and intelligently emerging, noisy and sovereign, risen quails, with a ring of remarkable virginity. His work has surpassed us, going as far as to leave us breathless, as though fogged in a lexicographic shiver of surprises.» The shiver, on the rebound and with delight, tickled Panets's spine, and his head grew another inch. «I already know I'm a poet, but that's not enough, dammit!» Amadeu, to motivate himself, said after some time had passed. And he chose four or five more activities, studious ones, and excelled in all of them: what material could he deny the majesty of his head? Ah, enough, enough I tell you all, what a handsome head Amadeu Panets had! Inch by inch it invaded every possible human activity. Technicians opposed him with useless reticence. «You don't understand,» said the envious technicians, stragglers on the Olympian road. «As if. With this head?» Panets exalted. And from the corners of the land everyone had already seen the cause of his head's height. «Look

here, I'm telling you: things are going to end badly for this guy,»
Quildet Nogueres, over the long haul, surmised. «He coasts by,
nevertheless,» the crowd began to realize. And doubts began pop-
ping up. «Well, maybe he does it a little too much. When all is
said and done, who is he?» the people questioned. Classifications
rained down. «A genius of logic,» one sector of opinion affirmed.
«He doesn't refine his ideas!» the technicians rebutted. «An orator,» said another rumor. «He never finishes anything off with a
period,» argued the technicians. «A formidable man of action,»
a third group offered up. «Action?» «That head is a hindrance!»
they said in protest. «Would you all deny that he's also a poet?»
the good-spirited daisies ostentatiously unfurled. «A vile one!»
discounted all the ungrateful protesters of the eternal and fluid
younger generation. «Who is he and what is he, then?» the people
asked, growing angry. «An Olympian, ladies and gentleman,»
Panets said, smiling as he clarified that for them. «Olympian?»
Efrem Pedagog, who in the meantime had become hepatic, ridi-
culed. «Certainly not! If he is Panets, it's Panets alone who walks
his head.» «We know a cure for his head,» the people said. And
a shower of stones was unleashed against that head that could
be seen from any distance, that unhideable head. Panets fell and
struggled with death for months and months, but the stones didn't
get the best of his eminent head. «I'm going out, you know?» Panets said, stable by now, to Semproniana. «It's been a while since
I've walked it, and it agrees.» «Wretched me!» the wife cried.
«You're treating it as though it were . . . » «Olympian, xst!» said
Panets, caressing it. «You first, pass, let's go,» he said sweetly to his
head. And he left. «I said things were going to end badly for this

guy,» Quildet surmised. «And to think that, if there were a cure, it would have been nothing but a case of stiff neck!» lamented, between her sobs, sad, fertile, legitimated Semproniana.

# French Quasi-Story of Samson, Rediscovered

*To Antoni San Juan, fulfilling an old promise.*

Framis's fat wife was in the small Isabelian salon, conversing about life with Quildet Nogueres. «Of an evident softness, but not at all appealing,» Quildet thought while speaking at length and looking her over. «Not appealing or not at all appealing: how would I have to put it if I had to write it now?» Quildet absentmindedly wondered. He scanned, with a little anguish, his memory of grammar, which was in eternal rebellion. «You contradict yourself, dear,» he heard Ophelia placidly assure him. «O, I would love to believe that you've lost the thread of your line of thought.» Having returned from a small mental obstacle race, Quildet turned red and laughed. «Pardon me,» Quildet lied. «Your radiant eyes, perhaps, are at fault.» Pleased, Framis's fat wife sprawled across the sofa and expressed a perfectly polite, intimate desire. «You are slightly afraid,» the lady said. «Sit down beside me, Nogueres, and overcome your *timidité*,» she commanded him. Quildet obeyed in silence—his ingenuity in an extremely human solution of continuity. «Soft,» Quildet returned to his thought after that inevitable pause. «Quite a worked and morbid maturity. She's never skimped on her sensory reception, nor on delicacy, and now, smooth and delicate before me, amidst softness and damask. Soft and delicate and, with everything, not appealing, or not at all appealing; what bad luck!» «It has to be confessed that your age is quite a difficult one,» the woman meanwhile said. «I tremble, on the one hand, at the incapacity to translate the world of experiences into action, and I believe, what's more, that the evils of the past can end up being repeated, *car voici de nouveau le goût de la mort entre mes dents*,» and Ophelia bit into a chocolate with the voluptuousness of great training. «In place of living we aspire to talk, and tyrannical prohibitions forbid us from doing so,» she continued. «What, then, are we left with, my friend, in these difficult times?» «Truly,» Nogueres, with much good sense, agreed. «And I didn't want to remind you, as it would end up being too vulgar, of the harshness of the contemporary economic battle. You would suffer knowing that for the majority of us, despite many, many *parvenus* having cars, simple subsistence is a problem.» «Hush!» the rich woman conceded, her eyes blank. «For example, I can't see our Secundina, the doorkeeper, without my heart coming dislodged, no exaggeration. And the artist of the lofts, please, with the girl, the old woman, and Letizia, that poor, generically tubercular girl?» «What do you mean by "generically tubercular"?» Quildet inquired. «I mean that Letizia, so imaginative and pure before, is today just a sick person, a sick person with an ambiguous diagnosis; there are handfuls of them,» Ophelia said. «It would depress us to confirm,» added

Quildet, «the effects of hardship on the fragility of our bodies.» Framis's fat wife shook. «Enough with the imprudent comments, Nogueres,» she sighed, and a small morsel of pearl backed up into her inner canthus. «Remember, dear, that we live—*hélas!*—only once.» Scolded, scrupulous, he then approached a more frivolous theme to temper the severity of the dark subject. «And the young Italian is the wife of the painter or the poet?» Quildet asked. «Certainly not: *maîtresse*, and have a good day,» Framis's fat wife enthused. «The other day Secundina confirmed that to me herself.» A few playful yelps interrupted the newly begun *causerie*. «Beloved perfection!» Ophelia, upon hearing them, exclaimed. «Oh, what a memory, mine! I had forgotten to tell you. He's returned: the prodigal son returned to me this afternoon from his adventure.» «I congratulate you for it,» the pacific interlocutor barely murmured, as the yelps became exhortative and urgent. «Open the door for him, *faites-moi la grâce*,» Ophelia sang childishly to herself. An irrepressible repugnance crossed Nogueres' face. «*Volontiers*,» acceded Quildet, chivalrously. «But your Pekingese has never been kind to me,» he reminded her. «Oh, no, he adores you! Open the door for him, *mon ami*,» she insisted. Resigned, a fatalist, Nogueres rose to comply with the tender order. A petulant canine curiosity entered like a flash of lightning and immediately began to commit vexatious indiscretions all around the legs of Nogueres's trousers. «Forget about uncle and focus on *maman*, Samson,» sweet-talked the lady. «I will give you bonbons and chicken, love, but stop these instinctive impulses for me, and don't ever escape again; I melt away with worry every time and get so skinny,» Framis's fat wife caressingly said. «Little animals also want affection,» she pointed out, spiritually and blatantly, to Nogueres. «Soft, decidedly soft,» Quildet repeated to himself. «I like your smell, and the skill with which you use your shoes to entertain astonishes,» Framis's fat wife remarked. «I have to go,» Nogueres suddenly announced. «Already. So soon?» Ophelia said, surprised. «Now that we've just undertaken the topic of life.» And, with Samson in her arms, she accompanied Quildet toward the exit, without suspecting—lacking foresight and inept at the interpretation of premonitory signs—that his departure, due to a few imponderable slights, was irrevocably definitive.

# Sembobitis

*To Jordi Elias i Campins, one-of-a-kind altruist, with vindictive thanks.*

Off to the side, where he rested from the extreme brightness of the afternoon, Salom saw a cart advance along the road. Slowly, at the ass's pace, the cart approached. One of those little junkman's bells marked the rhythm of the animal's efforts. He led a strange figure, seated at ease up top. Soon Salom could make out the figure well enough. It was an old man with a brown face and an extremely long white beard. To cover his head he wore a tall skullcap like an orthodox pope, but it was yellowish. He wore a type of very loose tunic of an ennobling greenish tone, with purplish fringes, and full of stitched repairs. The cart drew up to the observer.

«Sembobitis,» Salom yelled out as a welcome.

«Eh?» said the other. «Is there any rabbit hide?» he began to sing in an automatic voice. The cart stopped.

«Sembobitis, by God, don't make me an object of your curses,» Salom said as he rose to greet him. «Why are you here before me, enjoying yourself, disguised as a junkman? To me you were always a kind wizard. I've known you for a long time, don't you recall? When I was small, you joined King Balthazar in a race after a star. To frighten me, to amuse me during my long afternoons of illness, you endured a metamorphosis to cardboard, put up with being handled, without much respect, by a sad and febrile child. From the stage of the portable theater, you performed your pity with enormous dignity. You were Balthazar's advisor, lover of Belkis of Saba, and you presided with fairness over that madness under the Memphis sky. You discovered the miracle star and in great peace you showed it to Balthazar. The Black King broke the anachronistic spell and rode off after the splendid light. I know the details of your pilgrimage across the desert, all the way to the far-off portal. I listened to the lessons with which, at night, protected by the bonfires, when the caravan slept, you dictated your wisdom. I followed your learned disputes with Gaspar and the other old man, your companions on the final stages. Your pupil Balthazar was young and argued vehemently, but your stare imposed serenity upon him. The Black King was easily swayed by sudden impulses, by ingenuous thoughts. Sometimes he even prompted me to smile, just the smile of a lonely invalid. You don't know how I loved you, Sembobitis. I've been hoping for this day, Sembobitis, hoping to meet you, finally, in flesh and bone. And now that the miracle is realized, you deny your identity and disguise yourself as a junkman. But your clothes don't fool me. They're the same clothes that the cardboard Sembobitis wore—although a little more patched up, it's true.»

«Before moving on, I have to confess that I don't understand a thing you're going on about,» the other man, interrupting him, said. «My name is Antonet Quel·la, fairly well known across all of the plain and in the seaside towns. As far back as I can remember, I've had a lumpy face, much hair in my beard, and a weakness for rabbit skins. If that weren't the case, what would I boil in my cauldron? My parents didn't leave me—easy, boy!—a thing, no savings, not a drop of inheritance. I had to get a move on, you know? I made it through hunger and humidity, I could tell you a thousand stories. I had to make a fool of myself—I made this mask you see, from one corner to another, going after rabbit skins. At first, when they saw how I looked, the children stoned me, but being stubborn, in the end I made headway and now I'm popular. From a far hour away, people recognize the ring of my little bell. "Quel·la is coming," the neighbors hurry to say to each other. And I fill my sack with the skins of sacrificed rabbits. I'm telling you, sir, I take in—I alone—more business than all the rest together, in this line of work. It's always satisfying, sir.»

«Sembobitis,» Salom cried out to intervene. «I've run all afternoon across vine-strewn hills, through the pines that dominate the sea. Each hill, each pine tree, each shoot of vine, each bit of herb on my land, all of them have extremely concrete personalities. All afternoon I've cut across my homeland-like-none-other, the countryside of Sinera held in my eyes with neither sorrow nor force; this perfect countryside that will destroy me. My lips can name every corner. It's a countryside without fog, of low sun, of *sardanes* danced on hillsides fading in the distance. At times, lookout towers and agaves evoke memories of the vanished shadows of Algerian pirates. The breeze blows by the grates of reeds and lies down over the fennel and Monk's Pepper. A small cart climbed up-creek toward Remei, and I pondered how the hoes drew grooves in the crops, and I stopped to talk with friends in our own tongue, the tongue of farmers and aristocrats, that tongue that ought never to die. After, I descended to the beach, to contemplate, quite quietly, motionless, how the dolphins jump and slip away. I took a break from the plenitude of today, and that's when you arrived, Sembobitis. But you arrived transformed into a junkman, and I'd waited for this moment for so long! Reveal yourself as you truly are and make this day even more complete. We'll discover together, at dusk, the secret of the stars, and you'll teach me the ins and outs with your guide. Your little copper ass will lead us through the darkness, and the little bell will ring through all the drowsy marsh. It will overcome the silence of the farms, the dog barks, the *ric-ric* of the crickets, the splashing of the oars of boats being launched into the calmness of the water. Later, I'll tell you things about the countries on the other side of the sea. I have visited lands beloved by you, Sembobitis. Everything has changed so much that you wouldn't recognize it. Memphis is now just a murmur of palms. Will you grant me your attention, Sembobitis, or is it that you're angry at me without my suspecting it?»

«It seems to me, on top of everything you assure me you've done, that you've had a bit to drink.»

Salom thought this over for a moment, with a certain amount of admiration.

«Tubau,» Antonet Quel·la said to the ass, which, during their dialogue, hadn't brayed even once. «Tubau, don't pay him any mind: you'd end up nuts. He's not all there, poor guy. I've known him for years: Am I or am I not Antonet Quel·la, the junkman? And how! On the other hand, he doesn't have any rabbit skins to sell. What say we get on our way, Tubau, my child? It's getting dark, you've rested, we'll get there late, and you're faint-hearted and between two twilights, I've always known that. I'm not telling you to run away from this guy, don't get frightened, he's harmless. Just do as you think fit, Tubau, my child.»

Having talked everything over, the man approached the ass and won him over, cautiously, with a slight crack of his whip. The ass protested noisily, but obeyed. The old man spelled it out for Salom:

«First, you have to approach him with finesse, because he's shy and, if you don't, he'll plant himself down. Okay, fare thee well.»

«Sembobitis!» Salom still cried out after him.

«Rabbit skins, any rabbit skins?» sang Antonet Quel·la, the junkman.

Little by little the cart rode off down the road beyond.

# The Moribund Country

The country that had lost its soul sat facing the port with its hands empty, looking out sadly at the dead water, when I arrived. «I'll soon be like them,» it exclaimed, «I already see it, I express nothing, nothing of my authentic self. Soon I'll be like these waters, a mirror of indifference.» «No way!» I said back. «You are a great, a formidable country.» «What do you know about it?» cried the poor old country, slightly revived now—since nothing's so prone to short-lived revivals as a poor old country. «What do you know about it,» it said, falling once more into despair. «I'm a shadow, a carcass. You already see it; he was the center and the path of my glory,» it said, pointing at the port. «All of the ships that set off on their conquests, the wise laws of the sea, the proud flag, all of that came from him. Now, on the other hand, he's old and moribund like me. And his old age is covered, like mine, with backstage make-up. The cadence of my imperial tongue has been lost. Now it's screamed more than spoken, no sentences finished, steeled by swear-words, blasphemies, coarse, brutal gestures suitable for hominidae. I've been turned into a literary patois, into a Volapük with neither intimacy nor refinement, without nuance, hardened by cold, pedantic, enigmatic, unbearable words. No one reads it, and the writings a few people shape—generally speaking, they're rickety, shapeless, gray, with no personality, no rigor, not even craft, and often propose to do nothing more than serve bastard interests. Aliens to a tradition of profound culture and refinement, my children don't interest themselves in that spirit of things. Materialists that they are, they imitate the techniques of foreigners. And precisely now, moribund and exhausted, a mean grimace, I live on the strength of a grotesque masquerade, on the calculations of a few minds ambitious and quick to betray. I'm just an anachronistic medieval silhouette.» «No, you are a great country, a country of the future, dammit!» I interrupted. «A medieval silhouette? So what. Do you have any idea of the importance in that? Haven't you read Spengler, Berdiaev (or however it's transcribed from Cyrillic), among other as or more eminent essayists, the honest muddles of the press, the people who without blinking have contemplated a god or an other face to face, the skeptical debunkers of myths that passionately start up other, untouchable myths, the university-descendant hypercritics of the prophets? It's your time, the time of your sea, of your tongue, of your empire, of your glory, of your wisdom.» «The sharpest and most balanced in the world,» said a far-off and patriotic heart. «You're rich, you're cultured,» I continued. «What do you think of your dance?» «The most beautiful in the world,» cried out the heart. «And of your popular song?» «There's not another like it: la, la, la,» the heart sang. «And of your prosperous hospitals, your orderliness, your citizenly neatness, the kindness of the inhabitants of your countryside? You can't be satisfied any longer with shoddy work and filth, you can't shift shameless beggars around in cars any longer, you can no longer ignore what you've been ignoring. Everything has a limit, you've reached it, you don't have to dig deep for more effort. Moribund? Who possesses your health, your drive! Do you want proof of it? What more do you need than your great, anarchic, exemplary, pretentious, *nouveau riche*, comfortless city-hamlet?» «The best of them all,» exalted the heart. «That's true. It can't be denied that no other is as gutted, nor as eternally patched-up,» the country agreed. «Add to that the harsh acerbity of Lavínia's neighbors, and those residing in their sphere. Listen to them,» I said. «One can't live in this tribe,» said the voice of Efrem Pedagog. «What will the Korongos of Nubia think of us?» «*Hélas, hélas, la bêtise humaine!*» sang the harmonious throat of Pulcre Trompel·li. «We are a fifth-, maybe a sixth-tier country,» affirmed Ecolampadi Miravitlles with evident satisfaction. «The Germans organized a colossal competition not long ago. The theme to develop was: "African bases for cretinism in men and in towns." We ended up the winners.» «Us, champions? A single bit of good news!» the eminent poet Aina Cohen excitedly said.[13] «Do you not hear the nightingale singing for victory? There, in the house of the old folk, while the good old man

> *Listens to the sweet song of the small bird*
> *and weighs figs in the kingdom of sleep.*

---

13  I christened my character thus because I didn't believe it right to name her anything else: Aina Cohen, the model creation from *Mort de Dama*, the admirable novel by «Dhey,» the great Catalan writer from Mallorca, Doctor Llorenç Villalonga. –S.F..

*His venerable head grows drowsy*
*to the rhythm of simmering paellas.*

«Don't forget, brothers, that we are the chosen ones of Our Father,» added the smooth reciter, after releasing and receiving some enthusiastic applause. «Did you hear Aina, did you hear her? Are you not convinced now?» I asked the country. «Yes,» he said, relenting. «But I find myself so decrepit! It's so cold, everything is spinning, I'm dying!» he suddenly screamed. The heart attack struck like lightning, and I didn't have time to help him. His body fell with a splash in the calming waters, in a solitary place, and I was the only witness to the small event. «Am I going to get wet for him?» I wondered. «We'll find another soon enough that will stand out to us even more. I'm going to telegraph the news. It's more essential than trying to save him. What a journalistic hit this will be!» I thought, as I distanced myself from the spot. «What's this idiot saying,» my fellow citizens asked upon reading the telegram the following day. «What does it say? "Old country drowned yesterday in waters of port. Cadaver has not been identified." Here, the country died, hurrah! We have a country that dies on us. Wow, I want details about that.» That day the write-ups were churned out feverishly, and with their increase balanced the meager publishing industry: at least some fifty copies were sold from piles of newspapers in the language of our land, that language they later called, intelligently, with such delicate love, a vernacular.

*Barcelona, 1934 – 1935.*
*Revised in Sinera, August 1949 – July 1964. And in Lavínia,*
*October 1967 – July 1974 – December 1980 – July 1984*

SALVADOR ESPRIU (1913–1985) is considered one of the Catalan language's most significant postwar writers, producing fiction, poetry, and drama. Two volumes of his *Selected Poems* are available in English translation.

ROWAN RICARDO PHILLIPS is the author of *The Ground: Poems* as well as numerous essays, poems, and translations.

# SELECTED DALKEY ARCHIVE TITLES

FORD MADOX FORD,
*The March of Literature.*
JON FOSSE, *Aliss at the Fire.*
*Melancholy.*
MAX FRISCH, *I'm Not Stiller.*
*Man in the Holocene.*
CARLOS FUENTES, *Christopher Unborn.*
*Distant Relations.*
*Terra Nostra.*
*Vlad.*
*Where the Air Is Clear.*
TAKEHIKO FUKUNAGA, *Flowers of Grass.*
WILLIAM GADDIS, *J R.*
*The Recognitions.*
JANICE GALLOWAY, *Foreign Parts.*
*The Trick Is to Keep Breathing.*
WILLIAM H. GASS, *Cartesian Sonata*
*and Other Novellas.*
*Finding a Form.*
*A Temple of Texts.*
*The Tunnel.*
*Willie Masters' Lonesome Wife.*
GÉRARD GAVARRY, *Hoppla! 1 2 3.*
*Making a Novel.*
ETIENNE GILSON,
*The Arts of the Beautiful.*
*Forms and Substances in the Arts.*
C. S. GISCOMBE, *Giscome Road.*
*Here.*
*Prairie Style.*
DOUGLAS GLOVER, *Bad News of the Heart.*
*The Enamoured Knight.*
WITOLD GOMBROWICZ,
*A Kind of Testament.*
PAULO EMÍLIO SALES GOMES, *P's Three*
*Women.*
KAREN ELIZABETH GORDON, *The Red Shoes.*
GEORGI GOSPODINOV, *Natural Novel.*
JUAN GOYTISOLO, *Count Julian.*
*Exiled from Almost Everywhere.*
*Juan the Landless.*
*Makbara.*
*Marks of Identity.*
PATRICK GRAINVILLE, *The Cave of Heaven.*
HENRY GREEN, *Back.*
*Blindness.*
*Concluding.*
*Doting.*
*Nothing.*
JACK GREEN, *Fire the Bastards!*
JIŘÍ GRUŠA, *The Questionnaire.*
GABRIEL GUDDING,
*Rhode Island Notebook.*
MELA HARTWIG, *Am I a Redundant*
*Human Being?*
JOHN HAWKES, *The Passion Artist.*
*Whistlejacket.*
ELIZABETH HEIGHWAY, ED., *Contemporary*
*Georgian Fiction.*
ALEKSANDAR HEMON, ED.,
*Best European Fiction.*
AIDAN HIGGINS, *Balcony of Europe.*
*A Bestiary.*
*Blind Man's Bluff.*
*Bornholm Night-Ferry.*
*Darkling Plain: Texts for the Air.*
*Flotsam and Jetsam.*
*Langrishe, Go Down.*
*Scenes from a Receding Past.*
*Windy Arbours.*
KEIZO HINO, *Isle of Dreams.*
KAZUSHI HOSAKA, *Plainsong.*

ALDOUS HUXLEY, *Antic Hay.*
*Crome Yellow.*
*Point Counter Point.*
*Those Barren Leaves.*
*Time Must Have a Stop.*
NAOYUKI II, *The Shadow of a Blue Cat.*
MIKHAIL IOSSEL AND JEFF PARKER, EDS.,
*Amerika: Russian Writers View the*
*United States.*
DRAGO JANČAR, *The Galley Slave.*
GERT JONKE, *The Distant Sound.*
*Geometric Regional Novel.*
*Homage to Czerny.*
*The System of Vienna.*
JACQUES JOUET, *Mountain R.*
*Savage.*
*Upstaged.*
CHARLES JULIET, *Conversations with*
*Samuel Beckett and Bram van*
*Velde.*
MIEKO KANAI, *The Word Book.*
YORAM KANIUK, *Life on Sandpaper.*
HUGH KENNER, *The Counterfeiters.*
*Flaubert, Joyce and Beckett:*
*The Stoic Comedians.*
*Joyce's Voices.*
DANILO KIŠ, *The Attic.*
*Garden, Ashes.*
*The Lute and the Scars*
*Psalm 44.*
*A Tomb for Boris Davidovich.*
ANITA KONKKA, *A Fool's Paradise.*
GEORGE KONRÁD, *The City Builder.*
TADEUSZ KONWICKI, *A Minor Apocalypse.*
*The Polish Complex.*
MENIS KOUMANDAREAS, *Koula.*
ELAINE KRAF, *The Princess of 72nd Street.*
JIM KRUSOE, *Iceland.*
AYŞE KULIN, *Farewell: A Mansion in*
*Occupied Istanbul.*
EWA KURYLUK, *Century 21.*
EMILIO LASCANO TEGUI, *On Elegance*
*While Sleeping.*
ERIC LAURRENT, *Do Not Touch.*
HERVÉ LE TELLIER, *The Sextine Chapel.*
*A Thousand Pearls (for a Thousand*
*Pennies)*
VIOLETTE LEDUC, *La Bâtarde.*
EDOUARD LEVÉ, *Autoportrait.*
*Suicide.*
MARIO LEVI, *Istanbul Was a Fairy Tale.*
SUZANNE JILL LEVINE, *The Subversive*
*Scribe: Translating Latin*
*American Fiction.*
DEBORAH LEVY, *Billy and Girl.*
*Pillow Talk in Europe and Other*
*Places.*
JOSÉ LEZAMA LIMA, *Paradiso.*
ROSA LIKSOM, *Dark Paradise.*
OSMAN LINS, *Avalovara.*
*The Queen of the Prisons of Greece.*
ALF MAC LOCHLAINN,
*The Corpus in the Library.*
*Out of Focus.*
RON LOEWINSOHN, *Magnetic Field(s).*
MINA LOY, *Stories and Essays of Mina Loy.*
BRIAN LYNCH, *The Winner of Sorrow.*
D. KEITH MANO, *Take Five.*
MICHELINE AHARONIAN MARCOM,
*The Mirror in the Well.*
BEN MARCUS,
*The Age of Wire and String.*

WALLACE MARKFIELD,
  *Teitlebaum's Window.*
  *To an Early Grave.*
DAVID MARKSON, *Reader's Block.*
  *Springer's Progress.*
  *Wittgenstein's Mistress.*
CAROLE MASO, *AVA.*
LADISLAV MATEJKA AND KRYSTYNA
  POMORSKA, EDS.,
  *Readings in Russian Poetics:*
  *Formalist and Structuralist Views.*
HARRY MATHEWS,
  *The Case of the Persevering Maltese:*
  *Collected Essays.*
  *Cigarettes.*
  *The Conversions.*
  *The Human Country: New and*
  *Collected Stories.*
  *The Journalist.*
  *My Life in CIA.*
  *Singular Pleasures.*
  *The Sinking of the Odradek*
  *Stadium.*
  *Tlooth.*
  *20 Lines a Day.*
JOSEPH MCELROY,
  *Night Soul and Other Stories.*
THOMAS MCGONIGLE,
  *Going to Patchogue.*
ROBERT L. MCLAUGHLIN, ED., *Innovations:*
  *An Anthology of Modern &*
  *Contemporary Fiction.*
ABDELWAHAB MEDDEB, *Talismano.*
GERHARD MEIER, *Isle of the Dead.*
HERMAN MELVILLE, *The Confidence-Man.*
AMANDA MICHALOPOULOU, *I'd Like.*
STEVEN MILLHAUSER, *The Barnum Museum.*
  *In the Penny Arcade.*
RALPH J. MILLS, JR., *Essays on Poetry.*
MOMUS, *The Book of Jokes.*
CHRISTINE MONTALBETTI, *The Origin of Man.*
  *Western.*
OLIVE MOORE, *Spleen.*
NICHOLAS MOSLEY, *Accident.*
  *Assassins.*
  *Catastrophe Practice.*
  *Children of Darkness and Light.*
  *Experience and Religion.*
  *A Garden of Trees.*
  *God's Hazard.*
  *The Hesperides Tree.*
  *Hopeful Monsters.*
  *Imago Bird.*
  *Impossible Object.*
  *Inventing God.*
  *Judith.*
  *Look at the Dark.*
  *Natalie Natalia.*
  *Paradoxes of Peace.*
  *Serpent.*
  *Time at War.*
  *The Uses of Slime Mould:*
  *Essays of Four Decades.*
WARREN MOTTE,
  *Fables of the Novel: French Fiction*
  *since 1990.*
  *Fiction Now: The French Novel in*
  *the 21st Century.*
  *Oulipo: A Primer of Potential*
  *Literature.*
GERALD MURNANE, *Barley Patch.*
  *Inland.*

YVES NAVARRE, *Our Share of Time.*
  *Sweet Tooth.*
DOROTHY NELSON, *In Night's City.*
  *Tar and Feathers.*
ESHKOL NEVO, *Homesick.*
WILFRIDO D. NOLLEDO, *But for the Lovers.*
FLANN O'BRIEN, *At Swim-Two-Birds.*
  *At War.*
  *The Best of Myles.*
  *The Dalkey Archive.*
  *Further Cuttings.*
  *The Hard Life.*
  *The Poor Mouth.*
  *The Third Policeman.*
CLAUDE OLLIER, *The Mise-en-Scène.*
  *Wert and the Life Without End.*
GIOVANNI ORELLI, *Walaschek's Dream.*
PATRIK OUŘEDNÍK, *Europeana.*
  *The Opportune Moment, 1855.*
BORIS PAHOR, *Necropolis.*
FERNANDO DEL PASO, *News from the Empire.*
  *Palinuro of Mexico.*
ROBERT PINGET, *The Inquisitory.*
  *Mahu or The Material.*
  *Trio.*
A. G. PORTA, *The No World Concerto.*
MANUEL PUIG, *Betrayed by Rita Hayworth.*
  *The Buenos Aires Affair.*
  *Heartbreak Tango.*
RAYMOND QUENEAU, *The Last Days.*
  *Odile.*
  *Pierrot Mon Ami.*
  *Saint Glinglin.*
ANN QUIN, *Berg.*
  *Passages.*
  *Three.*
  *Tripticks.*
ISHMAEL REED, *The Free-Lance Pallbearers.*
  *The Last Days of Louisiana Red.*
  *Ishmael Reed: The Plays.*
  *Juice!*
  *Reckless Eyeballing.*
  *The Terrible Threes.*
  *The Terrible Twos.*
  *Yellow Back Radio Broke-Down.*
JASIA REICHARDT, *15 Journeys Warsaw*
  *to London.*
NOËLLE REVAZ, *With the Animals.*
JOÃO UBALDO RIBEIRO, *House of the*
  *Fortunate Buddhas.*
JEAN RICARDOU, *Place Names.*
RAINER MARIA RILKE, *The Notebooks of*
  *Malte Laurids Brigge.*
JULIÁN RÍOS, *The House of Ulysses.*
  *Larva: A Midsummer Night's Babel.*
  *Poundemonium.*
  *Procession of Shadows.*
AUGUSTO ROA BASTOS, *I the Supreme.*
DANIËL ROBBERECHTS, *Arriving in Avignon.*
JEAN ROLIN, *The Explosion of the*
  *Radiator Hose.*
OLIVIER ROLIN, *Hotel Crystal.*
ALIX CLEO ROUBAUD, *Alix's Journal.*
JACQUES ROUBAUD, *The Form of a*
  *City Changes Faster, Alas, Than*
  *the Human Heart.*
  *The Great Fire of London.*
  *Hortense in Exile.*
  *Hortense Is Abducted.*
  *The Loop.*
  *Mathematics:*
  *The Plurality of Worlds of Lewis.*

FOR A FULL LIST OF PUBLICATIONS, VISIT:
**www.dalkeyarchive.com**

# SELECTED DALKEY ARCHIVE TITLES

FOR A FULL LIST OF PUBLICATIONS, VISIT:
www.dalkeyarchive.com